RETURN TO CAPTIVA

CAPTIVA ISLAND

BOOK NINE

ANNIE CABOT

CABOT PUBLISHING GROUP

ISBN ebook, 979-8-9874624-8-5

ISBN paperback, 979-8-9874624-9-2

CHAPTER 1

Carrying three tall plastic cups of lemonade and a couple of balloons, Lauren Phillips struggled to get through the front door of her office building.

The parking lot was filled with people and the excitement was palpable.

Today was the Grand Opening of the new restaurant next door and everyone in the small plaza was celebrating.

Brian, Lauren's top real estate agent, opened the door and grabbed two cups.

"What in the world? Why didn't you send me over there? You shouldn't be carrying so much."

Lauren glared at him. "Being five months pregnant doesn't mean I'm ill, you know. I'm perfectly capable of carrying a few cups of lemonade."

Her assistant, Nell Hansen, took one of the cups from Brian. "What can you expect from a confirmed bachelor who has no plans to ever be a father?"

"That has nothing to do with it," Brian insisted. "You don't have to have children to have an opinion about pregnancy or anything else having to do with marriage and children," he insisted.

Lauren smiled and looked at Nell. "He's right, you know. Everyone is entitled to their opinion even if they don't know what they're talking about."

Nell laughed. "Hey, Brian, why don't you go next door and get a few balloons for your nieces and nephews. I bet they'd love to get a balloon from their favorite uncle," she teased.

"Keep your day job, Nell. A comedian you are not," he said.

"Nell, do you have those reports I asked for yesterday?"

"I put them on your desk."

"Great, thanks."

"Lauren, if you don't mind, I think I will go next door. I just want to see how they've done the place over," Nell said. Turning to Brian, she added, "Want to join me?"

Lauren smiled. "Go on, you two. They've got a few appetizers to go along with the lemonade."

Brian's face lit up. "Now you're talking."

Lauren loved listening to her two employees banter back and forth. They acted like children sometimes, but mostly, they were two of the finest and most dedicated people she'd ever worked with.

"We won't be long," Nell said as she and Brian walked out the front door.

As soon as they left, Lauren went into her office. When her phone rang, she smiled at seeing her mother's name.

"Hey, Mom. Are you and Chelsea in Key West yet?"

"We're just about to drive over the Seven-Mile Bridge. I thought I'd check in and see how you're feeling. Last time we talked you were having heartburn all the time."

Lauren nodded. "I still am, but now my ankles are starting to swell too. Isn't pregnancy wonderful?"

Maggie laughed. "I remember those days. The best part is when that little one is born. You know what I'm talking about."

"Oh, I know. I'm already in love with this little bundle, heartburn and all."

"Is there anything else I need to know about? How is your grandmother?" Maggie asked.

"She's excited about the move to Florida. It's all she talks about."

"I'm sure she complained that I've gone off with Chelsea instead of preparing for her arrival. Not that there's anything I really need to do," Maggie said.

Lauren laughed. "How did you know?"

"I know my mother."

"Well, she doesn't complain exactly. She just says that she can't wait for you to get back so she can move into her new place."

"Thanks for telling me. This trip to Key West will be all the more enjoyable knowing what I have to deal with when we get back. Anyway, I've got to go. You take care of you and that baby. Say hi to Jeff and the girls, and I'll call again."

"I will. Love you, Mom. Say hello to Chelsea."

Lauren loved that her mother was having so much fun. She hoped that her grandmother would find new friends when she moved to Florida. The last thing she wanted to see was her mother becoming an around-the-clock caretaker.

Lauren leaned back in her chair and thought about how much her family had gone through since her father's death. She had no illusions about what kind of husband her father was. That he was unfaithful and hurt her mother several times pained Lauren, but it didn't change the fact that he was still her father, and she loved him.

His death meant there would never be another opportunity for her to talk to him, leaving several unanswered questions that continued to haunt her.

As difficult as it was for her to accept her father's behavior when he was alive, Lauren's empathy for him grew the older she got. Still, forgiveness was a constant work in progress.

Lauren rubbed her stomach and thought about her baby. She and Jeff agreed not to find out the sex of the baby early, but she felt certain that this little one would be their first boy. She couldn't explain why, but deep inside she repeated her baby's name…Daniel.

Lauren kept her feelings to herself. She had no idea how the rest of the family would feel about her naming her new baby after their father. More than anything, she never wanted her child to feel ashamed of his name.

It was still too early in her pregnancy to make such a decision, and there was still the possibility that the baby could be a girl. However, she couldn't ignore the pull of her father's memory, and her desire to connect whatever was left of it with her child.

Lauren felt slightly nauseous which was a new second trimester experience. Her first two pregnancies were a breeze compared to this one. From the day she found out she was pregnant again, the morning sickness had been relentless and she was tired all the time.

She had several days where she felt great but then she noticed at the start of her fifth month that smells were particularly difficult for her once again.

Lauren worried that the restaurant next door would be a problem. Now, as she sat at her desk, her worst fears were realized. The restaurant's stone pizza ovens were constantly ablaze and the acrid smell of wood burning permeated her office.

Waves of nausea hit her and she tried not to vomit, but it was no use. Running to the bathroom, she then hovered over the toilet and held onto the wall for support. Everything she had eaten that morning along with the lemonade from next door came up.

Her throat burned and so she cupped her hand under the water faucet and rinsed the inside of her mouth. She looked at her reflection in the mirror and saw her face was white and her hair disheveled. She splashed water on her face and then wiped it with the paper towel. She took several deep breaths trying to compose herself.

When she emerged from the bathroom, she could see that a haze had filled the office, and her heart skipped a beat. Within seconds the haze turned into black smoke, and wind blew flames just outside the front windows.

Lauren's heart raced when she realized what was happening. She could barely make out the activity outside the building but could tell that the flickering lights meant that someone had called the fire department.

Her pulse quickened as she ran back to the bathroom. She pulled out several sheets of paper towels, dousing them in water. Covering her nose and mouth, she ran to her desk and grabbed her cellphone and purse and headed for the front door.

It was impossible to see where she was going and twice bumped into things. She could hear someone calling her name as panic grasped her chest. Fear consumed her and as she approached the front of the office, glass shattered, sending the shards toward her body.

She cradled her belly and fell to the floor. Feeling the sting and pain of the glass, she knew that she couldn't waste time trying to pull them from her skin. Terrified, she started to cry and screamed when someone reached for her, pushing the glass further into her body.

"You're all right. Come with me," a man said.

He wrapped his arms around her and pulled her close as he guided her out of the building and to safety.

"Wait! Please, I need to find Brian and Nell," she gasped as the man put an oxygen mask on her.

She didn't realize just how much she was fighting the very person who was trying to save her life.

"No! Stop. You have to find them. They were in the restaurant. Please," she screamed.

The fireman was kind and gentle but she could tell that he

remained firm and focused on getting her safely inside the ambulance.

"If they were in the restaurant, they'll find them. Don't worry. I need you to stay calm and lay back," he said.

There were several EMT personnel surrounding the stretcher doing their best to keep Lauren from getting up.

Once settled, Lauren watched the man who had saved her life run toward the building. Lauren looked up at a woman who was smiling down at her. The EMT put a stethoscope against Lauren's chest.

"I'm five months pregnant," Lauren said.

The woman placed her hand on Lauren's belly.

"You and your baby are going to be just fine," she answered.

Within seconds the ambulance pulled away from the parking lot and headed for the hospital. Lauren closed her eyes and said a silent prayer that Nell and Brian were safe. There wasn't anything more she could do.

Michael Wheeler had spent the better part of a year behind a desk at the police headquarters. Now, after a long period of rehabilitation and therapy, he returned to his usual detail and felt his life was back on track.

Sitting in his parked patrol car, he sipped his coffee and looked over at his partner's sandwich.

"Are you seriously going to eat that thing?" Michael asked.

"Why, what's wrong with it?" Jeremy asked.

"Wrong with it? It's bigger than your head."

"Hey, I'm a growing boy. I need to eat."

Michael laughed. "You're growing all right. Maybe not the way you'd like though."

Michael's cellphone rang and it was his wife Brea calling. "Hey honey, what's up?"

"Michael, there's a fire at Lauren's real estate office. It's really bad. The whole strip mall is destroyed."

"Where's Lauren? Is she all right?" he asked.

"I don't know. I called Jeff's phone but it went to voicemail. I know you're in Boston, but can you call someone up here? Maybe the Andover police?"

Michael was used to emergency calls, but not where his sister or family was concerned.

"Yeah, I'll call the station near there. Don't worry, I'm sure Lauren is safe. I'll call you when I know something."

Michael hung up and turned to Jeremy. "Who do we know in Andover?"

"I know Cliff Matthews is in Andover. He should know what's going on."

Michael nodded and let Jeremy make the call. They waited until Cliff answered the phone. Cliff's voice came through the speaker.

"Yeah, it's bad. Two people are dead and several others injured. At least those are the numbers right now. They expect that to increase. They've taken everyone to Andover General."

"Thanks, Cliff."

Jeremy looked at Michael. "What can we do?"

"I'm going up there. I've got to keep trying to reach my brother-in-law."

"Of course. Do you want me to go with you?"

Michael shook his head. "No. Thanks, buddy." He looked at the police station. "Let them know inside will you?"

Jeremy nodded. "Of course."

Jeremy gathered his sandwich and got out of the car. He leaned down and looked through the open window at Michael.

"Let me know if you need anything at all," he said.

"I will. Thanks."

Michael watched Jeremy walk into the building and then closed his eyes.

Please, God. Let her and the baby be okay.

He got out of the police car and into his own. Backing out onto the road, he took a deep breath and dialed Jeff's number. Jeff answered after one ring.

"Michael! Have you heard anything?"

"No, nothing just yet. All I know is that they've taken several people over to Andover General."

"Lauren was in the office when the fire broke out. I know for a fact that she wasn't showing any houses this morning, so she must have been inside. I'm out of my mind. I'm headed to the hospital. Are you coming up?"

"Yeah, I'm on my way. Listen, everything is going to be ok. Please don't think the worst. I'll meet you there."

Michael could hear Jeff crying through his words.

He was about to hang up when Jeff stopped him.

"Michael, two people are dead. If Lauren and the baby are gone..."

Michael swallowed. "I know, man, but you have to stay positive. Lauren and the baby are fine. Hang in there. Do you hear me? They are going to get in touch with you any minute. You'll see. You hang up the phone and I'll be with you soon."

Michael ended the call and repeated the same encouragement aloud. He needed to convince himself as much as he did Jeff, and in his heart he believed his sister and her baby were alive.

There was nothing he could do but will it to be so, and so, for the next thirty minutes, driving through the north of Boston, that was exactly what he did.

CHAPTER 2

Every day, from nine to noon, Devon Hutchins scheduled his meetings, looked through the stacks of papers on his desk, and called his sons Trevor and Clayton into his office to go over their latest development project before heading out to oversee construction.

By one o'clock when he had done none of these things, his assistant, Christina, called Devon's home looking for him. The housekeeper answered the call and said that she hadn't seen Mr. Hutchins that morning but assumed he had gone into the office.

When Christina failed to locate Devon, she called Trevor.

"I haven't heard from him this morning either. I agree it's unusual, but everyone is entitled to a day off occasionally. I'll look into it. Thanks, Christina."

Trevor hung up the phone and walked to his brother Clayton's office.

"Hey, have you talked to Dad this morning?"

Clayton shook his head. "No. I was just coming to ask you the same thing," Clayton answered. "Do you think he's taking the day off?"

Trevor shrugged. "I guess it's possible, but have you ever remembered him doing that and not telling anyone?"

"The truth is that I don't even remember him taking a day off…period."

Clayton reached for his cellphone.

"I'll call Mom. What are the odds that she's sitting in a spa getting a facial, pedicure or spending tons of money on the latest Chanel suit? How about we bet on it? I say, she's at the spa. What do you say? You can put your money right here on my desk."

If Trevor wasn't so worried about their father, he might have taken the bet.

"Knock it off. Just call her, will you?"

Clayton dialed her number and put her on speaker phone.

"Mom! Hey, we haven't seen Dad this morning and wondered if you knew where he was."

"I have no idea where your father goes when he leaves the house. I only assume he goes to work because the money keeps coming in."

Clayton smiled and looked over at Trevor who rolled his eyes. "Mom, are you home now?"

"Yes, I'm outside by the pool. I've got a hair appointment in an hour so I can't talk for long."

Losing patience with his mother, Trevor shook his head. "Can you please just look outside to see if his car is still in the driveway?"

Their massive mansion had a four-car garage, but for some reason, their father insisted on parking his Mercedes as close to the front door as possible.

"Fine. Hang on."

They could hear their mother's heavy sigh and smiled, knowing they'd upset her morning routine.

The next sound they heard was their mother screaming for the housekeeper to call 911.

They could hear her yelling, "Devon! Devon! Please, don't leave me."

"Mom!" Clayton yelled into the phone. "What's happening?"

There was a muffled noise and what Trevor assumed was their mother's fumbling for the phone.

"Your father is dead. I think he's dead. He's on the floor and not moving."

"Mom, calm down. Is he breathing?" Trevor asked.

She didn't answer.

"Mom!" Clayton yelled. "Mom! Did Alana call 911?"

"Yes…yes, he's breathing. Yes, she called. I can already hear the sirens."

Trevor ran his hand through his hair. "Just stay with him. The paramedics will know what to do."

They could hear Eliza Hutchins calling for her husband through her crying, and then her talking to the emergency medical people. Trevor and Clayton stayed on the phone waiting for their mother to come back to the phone.

"They're taking him to the hospital, and I'm going to drive there behind them. I've got to go."

"Cape Coral Hospital?"

"Yes. Boys, please hurry. He's alive right now, but I don't know how long he'll hold on."

"We're on our way," Trevor answered.

Clayton looked at Trevor. "My car is right out front. I'll drive," he said.

They got inside the car and Clayton hit the gas pedal hard.

Trevor's mind raced with questions. "Do you think it was a heart attack?"

Clayton shrugged. "I have no idea. I mean, it sounds like that, doesn't it?"

Trevor nodded.

They drove in silence for several minutes before Trevor said what he'd been thinking. Shaking his head, he said, "Dad's always seemed larger than life. It's impossible to think that he could die. I realize that we all die, but…not him…not him."

"I know what you mean. He's a tough guy. He's strong. He'll make it. We can't think of him dying."

"Absolutely, you're right. He'll be fine."

Trevor wasn't sure he believed what he was saying, but what he did believe was that if anyone could skirt death, it was Devon Hutchins.

Lauren lay on a table in the emergency room, as the attending physician and nurses worked to remove the shards of glass from her body.

Everything they did was to not only secure the safety of her pregnancy, but to keep her as calm as possible without sedation. Once the glass was removed and the wounds cleaned, the plan was to admit her overnight for observation.

Somewhere in all the confusion, Lauren lost her cellphone and purse and had to assume they were lost in the fire. She tried to stay calm for the baby's sake, but she couldn't feel totally at peace until she knew what had happened to Nell and Brian.

Jeff was at the foot of her bed and moved to her side as soon as the doctors left. He couldn't wrap his arms around her because of the bandages, but he put his hand on her face and kissed her.

"Thank God you're okay. What happened?"

Lauren shook her head. "I honestly don't know. I have to assume the fire started at the restaurant, but I have no idea. Nell and Brian went next door because of the grand opening. I was in the bathroom and when I came out I saw the smoke and fire. I tried to get to the front of the building but the smoke was too much. I covered my face with wet paper towels. It was all I had."

Michael arrived just as they were about to bring Lauren upstairs. "Hey, sis."

"Michael! What are you doing here?"

"Honey, the fire is all over the news. Of course, Michael was going to hear about it," Jeff said.

Lauren smiled. "Of course, stupid me. I'm so glad you're both here."

Michael leaned down and kissed Lauren. "What can Brea and I do to help? What about the girls? We can take them over to our house."

"That would be great. I want to be here at the hospital with her. They're at school right now, but they get out at three o'clock. Do you think you or Brea can pick them up?" Jeff asked.

"Absolutely. I'll call Brea. She's anxious for me to call her with an update."

Lauren grabbed Michael's arm. "Before you go, can you please check around and find out about my employees? Nell Hansen and Brian Donohue. They were inside the restaurant when the fire started. I don't know if they got out."

"Let me go see. Someone should know something. I'll be right back," Michael answered.

Lauren pulled Jeff close. "Why didn't the sprinklers or the smoke alarm go off? Something doesn't make sense. They had the inspectors in when they finished with the construction next door," she asked.

"Did anyone meet with the other tenants? Did they talk to you these last few months?"

Lauren shook her head. "No. No one got in touch with me."

Jeff seemed pensive.

"What are you thinking?" she asked.

He shook his head. "I'm not sure what I'm thinking, except that someone dropped the ball here and I plan to find out who and how this could happen."

Michael returned and Lauren searched his face for any emotion. He shook his head. "Nothing. No one knows anything about them."

Lauren started to cry. "They know something. They're just not telling us. They're dead. I know it."

She put her hands over her face and let the tears fall.

"No. Honey, stop. You can't give up hope. Please, don't cry."

Just then a nurse came into the room with a larger bed. "We're ready to move you upstairs. If you two gentlemen would step out for a minute. You can follow us to her room in a few minutes. She's going to room number three-twelve."

Jeff leaned down and kissed Lauren's cheek. "We'll be on the other side of the curtain."

Two nurses helped Lauren onto the hospital bed and wheeled her out into the open area. As they made their way out to the elevators, she saw Nell and Brian and the firefighter who saved her life walking toward her.

"Lauren! Thank God. We looked everywhere for you. Finally, someone told us that you were here," Nell said.

Lauren cried tears of joy seeing her friends as they were ready to hug her.

"Don't touch her you guys. They just pulled a bunch of glass out of her legs and arms," Jeff said.

Laughing, Lauren said, "Don't worry, just as soon as I can, I plan to squeeze the two of you as tightly as I can. What happened to you guys? I was screaming for you and even yelled at this nice man to get you out of there."

"Let me tell you about your friends. They saved a woman who was trapped inside. The woman was paralyzed with fear, but instead of running out of the building to save their own lives, they stayed with her until we arrived," the man said.

Lauren couldn't believe what she was hearing. "Anyone would have done the same thing in that situation," Brian responded.

"What is your name, sir?" Lauren asked.

"Bill Davis."

Lauren extended her hand to him. "Nice to meet you Bill. Thank you for saving my life."

"You're very welcome. I've got to meet up with a few people to give my report, but I'm glad that you're okay and that you've found your friends."

Bill Davis walked away and they continued to Lauren's room.

"I'll see you all upstairs. I've got to check on something," Jeff said.

Lauren watched her husband walk toward Bill Davis. She instinctively knew that they'd be talking about the sprinkler and smoke detector situation. Lives had been lost that day, and there would be further investigation of exactly what happened.

Her real estate business wouldn't be running for a while, but for her and her family, what mattered most was that Nell, Brian, and she and her baby survived the tragedy.

Lauren didn't yet know how many perished in the fire, and no amount of blame would ever bring them back. Still, they needed to know why the fire started and how they could prevent something like this from ever happening again.

"You know once we get you settled into your room, you're going to have to call Mom," Michael said.

Lauren nodded. "I know I have to call her at some point, but I hate to ruin her vacation. She and Chelsea are driving to Key West."

Michael smiled. "It's up to you, but you and I know that you're going to have to weigh which is worse...upsetting her now or having her really mad at you for not calling her."

Lauren nodded. "Good point."

"Here we are, room three-twelve. This will be your home away from home for the next twenty-four hours," the nurse said.

Once they got Lauren into her new bed, Michael leaned down and gave her a kiss on the forehead. "I'm going to head home. Brea and I will pick up Olivia and Lily."

"Thank you, Michael. Can you stop at the house and have the girls pick up what they need for school tomorrow? I'm sure they'll have homework, so make sure they do it and not sit in front of the television instead. You've got a key to our house, right?"

Michael nodded. "Yup. We're good. I'll have the girls call Jeff's phone after dinner."

"Oh, would you? That would be great. I assume my phone died in the fire. I can't wait to hear their voices. Thank Brea for us."

"Will do," he said. He looked at Nell and Brian. "Glad you two are okay."

"Thanks, Michael. Good to see you again," Brian said.

Jeff met Michael at the door. "I'm going to get the girls and I'll have them call you after dinner so they can talk to Lauren. You two hang in there, and don't hesitate to call if there is something else you need us to do."

Jeff shook Michael's hand. "Thanks so much, Michael."

Michael left and Jeff sat next to Lauren's bed. "How's my girl doing?"

"I'm fine. I haven't looked in the mirror, but do I look like Brian and Nell? I mean, do I have smoke soot all over my face?"

They all laughed, and Jeff put his hand on Lauren's face. "You've never looked more beautiful."

CHAPTER 3

"He's had a stroke."

Unprepared for those words, Eliza Hutchins clutched her son's shirt and leaned on him for support.

Trevor put his arm around his mother and focused on the doctor's words.

"The stroke impacted the right side of his brain which is why there is some paralysis on the left side of his body."

"Is it permanent?" Trevor asked.

"It's too soon to tell, but it is possible. More likely it's a temporary thing, but we won't know until we run more tests."

"Can I see my husband?" Eliza asked.

The doctor nodded. "You can. However, don't expect him to be able to talk to you. I know it's frustrating but it's more frustrating for him. He knows what he wants to say and he'll try, but what comes out won't make sense. I'd advise you to stress to him that he should rest and not try to talk, at least for now."

"Thank you, Doctor," Trevor said.

Clayton was on the other side of the room, seemingly uninterested, but Trevor knew better. His brother couldn't handle hospitals or illness of any kind. Coupled with the fact that he adored their father, Trevor understood that among their family members, Clayton would be the most devastated if their father died.

Trevor walked over to Clayton who was looking out the window at the street below.

"I'm going to take Mom inside. Do you want to come with us?"

His response hesitant, Clayton said, "Yeah, okay."

The three of them went into Devon's room just as the nurse was leaving.

Other than a picc line and fluids dripping into his right arm, Devon Hutchins had no tubes or machines surrounding his bed. His eyes were closed and he looked peaceful.

Trevor pulled a chair to the side of the bed so that his mother could sit as close as possible. The large private room had several chairs for guests but Clayton chose to stand at the foot of his father's bed. Trevor felt awful for his brother and wondered if it would have been better to not have him here.

Eliza spoke to her husband in soft, comforting words. "I'm here, my love. You have to rest and then, when you're feeling better, we'll take you home. You need a vacation anyway. I think just as soon as you are better we'll sit by the pool and relax for a few weeks," she said.

Devon opened his eyes and looked at his wife. He tried to talk but nothing came out.

"No, don't try to talk right now. You need to rest," she said.

Devon looked down at the end of his bed.

"Hey, Pop," Clayton said.

His father then looked at Trevor, lifted his right arm and pointed at him.

"Dad, you've had a stroke. You're going to get better, but you have to rest now. Don't try to talk. Conserve your energy so that you can get better fast," Trevor said.

Frustrated, Devon put his arm down and closed his eyes. There wasn't much they could do but let him sleep. They stayed in his room for another hour before Trevor put his hand on his mother's shoulder.

"Mom," he whispered. "We should go home. You need to eat something and then rest. We'll come back tomorrow."

"No. I want to stay with him," she answered.

Trevor understood his mother's desire to be with her husband but remained firm in his advice.

"He needs to sleep, and you need to let him rest. I'll drive you back here first thing in the morning. I promise. Come now, let's leave him to rest and let the doctors do whatever tests they need to do."

His mother nodded and got up from her chair. She leaned down and kissed her husband on his forehead.

"I'll be back tomorrow, honey. You rest. I love you."

When they got downstairs in the hospital lobby, Trevor took his mother's keys. Eliza looked frail and not at all like the strong woman Trevor had known all his life.

"I'm driving you home. Clayton can get back with his car. I want to stay with you for a bit."

She didn't fuss or disagree and Trevor was truly worried about her.

"I'll catch up with you later," Clayton said. "Mom, you rest and we'll talk tomorrow."

Eliza nodded. "Thank you, boys. I don't know what I'd do without you. Clayton, will you call Jacqui, Carolyn and Wyatt? I haven't talked to your sisters or Wyatt in about three weeks. I know they're busy with their own lives, but I think it's important that we get in touch. I pray that your father will get better, but..."

"Mom, stop. Dad is going to get stronger as the days pass. We just have to give him time," Trevor said.

"Trevor's right. I'll call them, but I'm not going to paint a bleak picture. Dad is going to improve and will be his old self, you'll see."

Trevor was more of a realist than Clayton, but that didn't

matter right now. He'd pretend that everything would be as it was for the sake of the family and his father's recovery. However he wasn't fooling himself. As strong as his father was, Devon Hutchins might have finally come up against something even he couldn't control.

Chelsea Marsden stood on the sidewalk and couldn't believe the size of the crowd on Duval Street. She was used to a steady stream of tourists just outside her home on Captiva Island, but Key West seemed more like Bourbon Street during New Orleans Mardi Gras.

"I hope my sisters know what they've gotten into," she said, watching her best friend Maggie Moretti beaming from ear to ear.

"I didn't think it was possible to feel more on vacation than I do back at home on Captiva, but this is awesome," Maggie said. "Why haven't we come down here sooner?"

Chelsea shrugged. "Oh, I don't know. Maybe because we've been dealing with family drama from the moment you moved to Florida?"

"Well, I don't know about you, but I plan to have fun while we're here."

"I have no argument with you on that but let's not forget the reason we're here," Chelsea reminded Maggie. "My sisters are going to flip when they realize that I've followed them here to give them money and apologize for being such a jerk."

"They're going to be thrilled to see you, Chelsea."

Chelsea looked at Maggie's purse. "Why is your phone constantly buzzing? Shouldn't you answer it?"

Maggie pulled her phone from the purse. "It's nothing important. I have news alerts from the WCVB app. Whenever something big is going on in Massachusetts, I get these breaking news alerts. To be honest, these days, it seems like everything is a breaking news story."

Maggie froze when she looked at her phone.

"What is it?" Chelsea asked.

"There's been a fire in Andover. It looks like…it couldn't be," Maggie said.

"What? Let me see that," Chelsea said as she pulled the phone from Maggie's hand.

Chelsea's heart skipped when she looked closer. "Oh, Maggie. It's the strip mall where Lauren's real estate office is located."

Maggie grabbed the phone. "It can't be. One of the kids would have called me by now. I'm calling Lauren's cellphone."

Maggie dialed Lauren's number. She looked at Chelsea and shook her head. "She's not answering. I'm trying Jeff."

Chelsea watched as Maggie called Jeff. "Same thing. No answer."

"Well, whatever you do, don't call your mother. Try Michael. He'll know if something is wrong."

Maggie nodded and dialed Michael's cellphone. By the time he picked up, Maggie was breathless.

"Michael, the news just came through my phone. Was the fire in Andover at Lauren's place?"

"Mom, Lauren is perfectly fine. Yes, it was the strip mall where her place is. She, Nell and Brian got out and they're fine."

"How did this happen?" Maggie asked.

"They're still investigating, but the new restaurant is most likely to blame. They just don't know yet."

Chelsea rubbed Maggie's back. She felt helpless to do more.

"Michael, I've tried both Jeff and Lauren's phones. They're not answering. Any idea why that is?"

Chelsea couldn't hear what Michael was saying, but the look on Maggie's face meant there was trouble.

"What?" Maggie screamed. "The hospital? I thought you said that she got out."

Chelsea leaned against the building and tapped her foot. Her anxiety building, she hated not knowing what Michael was telling Maggie.

"All right. Yes, of course, that makes sense. Can you please call Sarah and let her know? I won't be able to talk to her right now and I don't want her to be left out of the loop. Please tell Lauren that I want to hear from her or Jeff just as soon as they can call me. I'm going to be worried sick, so you tell them…yes, fine. I'm not hysterical. My daughter and her unborn child are in the hospital bandaged to the hilt, I'm entitled to be a little frantic."

Michael must have continued to reassure Maggie for the next few minutes, but when they were done talking, Maggie explained everything to Chelsea.

"Oh, Maggie. How terrifying. Thank heavens they got out in time."

Maggie turned to look at Chelsea. "Is there a dark cloud following me around that I can't see?"

Chelsea shrugged. "Maggie, if you're living, then you're going to have troubles. That's just life."

"Go on and preach to me. I know that. What I don't understand is why these challenges keep popping up. Maybe I did something really bad in a past life and I'm paying for it in this one."

Chelsea laughed. "I doubt it. Knowing you, any past lives you've had would have involved caring for everyone around you and completely ignoring your own needs. You're just going to have to accept that most things are out of your control. I heard once that if you can go with Plan B when Plan A doesn't work, you'll be a much healthier and happier person."

Maggie smiled. "In other words…adjust, right?"

Chelsea nodded. "Pretty much. Roll with the punches, Maggie Moretti. Right now, we first say a prayer of thanks that Lauren and her employees didn't die in that fire. After that, we need to figure out how to get to my sisters' place. Did you find Greene Street yet?"

Maggie looked at her phone. "GPS says we go left and walk about three blocks."

Chelsea's heart beat faster the closer they got to the Airbnb. She'd made a fool of herself when her sisters visited Captiva a few weeks earlier. Her visit to Key West was to make amends and support their desire to start a business here.

To calm her nerves Chelsea did as she always did…she made a joke.

"I expect to get a call from Lauren before you do," Chelsea teased.

"Oh? Why is that?"

"Because she'll want to thank me for keeping you occupied and for taking you as far south as possible. After all, Maggie, you and I both know that you're itching to call your children, send out a Code Red alarm and get on a plane to Massachusetts as fast as possible. Now that I've kidnapped you to Key West, I've made that fairly impossible."

Maggie shrugged. "Not impossible. Have you ever heard of a little thing called a taxi? I could make my way to Massachusetts if I really wanted to."

Chelsea understood Maggie's desire to be with her grown children whenever they needed her, but she also knew that the Wheeler family was large and loving and Lauren's siblings would be by her side throughout this latest ordeal.

"All kidding aside, I admire your restraint, Maggie. I know how difficult this is for you not to be with Lauren."

Chelsea looked off at the beautiful water to her left. She was never very good at sharing her innermost feelings, but Maggie needed to hear what was on her mind and heart.

"Thank you for being with me. I know you'd rather be with your daughter," Chelsea said.

Maggie stopped walking and grabbed Chelsea's arm.

"You've seen me through the most difficult times in my life. It's not too much to ask me to do the same for you. Not to mention that I'm truly blessed to have such a close family. I know that Christopher, Michael, Beth and Jeff will be by her side, and I'll know when and if Lauren needs her mother."

Chelsea smiled at Maggie's words. It was true that their friendship was the rock that Chelsea counted on in difficult times. Whatever lay ahead for her and her sisters, Chelsea felt that Maggie Moretti was her sister in the truest sense of the word.

CHAPTER 4

Exhausted, Trevor walked through the front door of his house and tried to perk up when Sarah came running to him.

"You wouldn't believe the morning I've had," she said. "The minute you left for work, Noah started coughing and sneezing and felt warm to the touch. Sure enough, he's got a fever. I called the doctor and he just said fluids, rest and Tylenol and to bring Noah in to see him if he gets any worse. Then Sophia began coughing, except I realized pretty early on that she's trying to imitate her brother. She's fine. She's just pretending so she can be just like Noah."

Sarah looked at her watch. "Hey, I just realized what time it is. What are you doing home so early?"

Trevor pulled Sarah close. "Dad had a stroke. He never came into the office so Clayton and I called the house. Mom found him on the floor."

"Oh no. Is he...?"

Trevor shook his head. "He's alive, but the next few days are crucial. It's impossible to tell if he's going to pull through."

"Oh, honey, I'm so sorry. Devon is a strong man. If anyone can beat this, it's him. How is your mother doing?"

"In shock, I think. She's never been a particularly independent person. The thought that my father might die and leave her...I don't know."

"Listen, it's not going to come to that. He's going to recover. You and your siblings have to think of it that way. If your mother is struggling, I think it will help her if you all stay positive."

Trevor sighed and nodded. "I know you're right, but...you should see him, Sarah, he looks so weak. He doesn't look strong at all. Mom asked Clayton to call Carolyn, Jacqui and Wyatt to let them know, but I think I'm going to have to talk to Wyatt myself."

"Oh? Why's that?"

Trevor sat on the sofa and ran his hand through his hair. "Dad always talks about wanting Wyatt to come back to work with him. It's his dream that all of his sons would work side-by-side with him. I know it's a stretch, but I'd like to make that happen for Dad. I don't know how I'll accomplish it, but I guess the first step would be to ask Wyatt to help Clayton and me while Dad is out."

Sarah nodded. "It's a good idea to present it as a temporary thing. Then, if God forbid your father does pass away, Wyatt might stay on permanently."

Trevor nodded. "That's my thinking. I asked Clayton to call Carolyn and Jacqui and I told him that I'd get in touch with Wyatt."

"Did you tell Clayton why you wanted to talk to Wyatt? I can't imagine he's too thrilled with the idea of your brother joining the company again. If you remember, Clayton wasn't all that thrilled when you decided to work for your father."

"You're right about that, but I think Clayton knows his limitations and the truth is Wyatt knows how to run a business, when he wants to that is. His problem is that he's been treated like a child his whole life, and so that's how he behaves. It gets him what he wants, so I guess he thinks, why change things?"

"What do you think Wyatt will say when you ask him to come home?"

Trevor shrugged. "I don't know. If I had to guess, I'd say his initial answer would be no. It's more complicated than that though. As much as I want Wyatt to act like a grown man, I honestly wonder if he's capable of it, and if not, then what? I'd like to think that Dad's illness might be the thing that motivates Wyatt to finally act responsibly."

"Do you and Clayton really need Wyatt?" Sarah asked.

"Probably not but imagine if it worked out…imagine the three Hutchins brothers together again. We could really make the family business soar. What I want is the same thing Dad wants. All of us together again. I don't know when needing that kicked in, and I know that Wyatt has issues with our father but so did I and look where we are now."

Sarah put her hand on Trevor's shoulder. "We never know what can happen in the blink of an eye. Your father's stroke might actually change the family dynamic for the better." She pulled him close. "And I know you. Your heart is big enough to accomplish anything. Even helping Wyatt to heal just as you did."

Sarah watched Trevor through the window. While the kids were napping, he went for a swim to decompress. Their house was right on the water, and as a family, the beach was their oasis from the stresses and hectic day-to-day pressures.

She was glad that her mother lived close but missed her siblings who lived back in Massachusetts. It had been a while since she'd last visited them and had recently wondered if a trip up north was in order.

Now that her father-in-law was ill, and her husband's responsibilities at work would soon increase, leaving Florida anytime soon was out of the question.

Her phone dinged on the table behind her, interrupting her thoughts. She could see that she had a message from her brother Michael asking her to call him back as soon as possible.

She dialed his number and when he answered the phone, she could tell right away that something was wrong.

"Michael, what is it?" she asked.

"It's Lauren. The strip mall and her agency had a fire. Lauren was slightly injured but not from the fire. She got out but the entire strip mall is gone."

"The baby? How's the baby?"

"The baby is fine," he answered.

"I've got to call Mom. She and Chelsea are in Key West."

"Mom knows. I called her."

Sarah sighed. "I assume she's already on a plane to Massachusetts?"

Michael laughed. "No, I don't think so, but that didn't stop her from barking instructions on the phone."

"Well, can you blame her? Mom still suffers guilt for being fifteen-hundred miles away from most of her children and grandchildren. I can't wait until Grandma gets down here. She'll demand a lot of Mom's focus. That should direct some of it away from us kids."

"Good point," he said. "How are things with you and your family?"

Sarah sat at the kitchen table. "Oh, that. Well, I guess when it rains it pours. Trevor's father had a stroke this morning. Eliza found him on the floor. He's in the hospital and it's pretty touch and go right now. All we can do is pray."

"I'm sorry to hear this. Please tell Trevor that we'll be praying up here too, and you text me if you need to talk."

"Thanks big brother. Do you think I should call Lauren?"

"I wouldn't right now. I'm not sure but I think she said something about losing her phone in the fire. If you call anyone it should be Jeff. I'd call tomorrow."

"Will do." She felt on the brink of tears. "Michael, if you talk to her before I do, please tell her I love her and am sending healing vibes from Florida."

"I'll tell her, honey. Don't worry. She's going to be fine."

They ended the call and Sarah went to the window once more. She watched Trevor dive under the water and resurface several times before walking back toward their house.

She was glad that he had something to do that would calm his nerves. With a sick child and two smaller ones demanding her attention, her new worries made relaxing impossible, but it didn't matter. All she wanted to do was hold her children and her husband and never let them go.

CHAPTER 5

Wyatt Hutchins was the spitting image of his brother Trevor and that fact annoyed him. Trevor was always considered the good son, the one who cared about people, humanity and the underdogs of the world.

Wyatt loved money, fast cars, and women. The more money he made from his hedge fund, the more he traveled the world with gorgeous women on his arm.

When he was younger he worked alongside his father but it didn't take him long before he'd miss days at work and refuse to take his job seriously.

He always knew that his father preferred Trevor and wanted him to join the family business. Since Trevor had other plans, Wyatt worked to get his father's approval and love until it became clear no amount of effort on his part would change how his father treated him.

Frustrated, Wyatt went out of his way to force his father's hand and make him fire him. He got his wish when he failed to show up for work for an entire week. Devon had enough of his son's attitude, but instead of teaching him to be a good man, he threw money at the problem.

Once on his own, Wyatt found other ways to make money and finally settled in the finance industry where he worked his way up to a position of importance, at least in his mind. He was more than happy to maintain his mid-level position by managing a hedge fund that had done quite well. For a while people thought he had talent, but his lack of a strong work ethic got him demoted and so he now depended entirely on his father's name and money.

He'd done most everything he could to stay as far removed from his father's real estate business empire, but he always knew that at some point his father would once again put pressure on his return to the family business.

He'd spent the last few years traveling the globe, dating women who were only interested in his good looks, celebrity connections, and enormous wealth.

Wyatt knew it and didn't care. His lavish lifestyle provided both his men and women friends with trips via the family's private jet, time on the family's yacht anchored in the south of France and parties at the family home in Aspen. The Hutchins family members hardly ever came to Colorado, so Wyatt took up residence there. He often joked that the place was usually filled with people who had come for a party and stayed for weeks after it was over.

He had come home a few years earlier for a family event but rarely showed up in Cape Coral or West Palm Beach to see his parents, and never heard from any of his siblings. Now, it appeared that a phone call from his brother Trevor might change his life once again, and this time not for the better.

"You have to come home, now. Dad had a stroke and might not make it," Trevor explained.

Wyatt knew this call was coming. He didn't know exactly when it would come, but he knew that Devon Hutchins was getting older and paid little attention to his diet and never exercised.

"Is that what the doctor said…that he might not make it?"

"Not in those words. He said the next couple of days were crucial and that they'd know more after additional tests. Right now Dad can't talk and he's paralyzed on one side of his body. The point is that Dad isn't going to be able to work for a while, no matter what his prognosis is. I think as the oldest son you might feel some obligation."

"What does that mean?" Wyatt asked.

"It means that it's Dad's money that has been supporting your way of life all these years. Don't you think you should come home and try to help the very business that makes your life what it is?"

Wyatt sat up straight. "Are you threatening me? Because if you are, Dad and I had an arrangement and…"

Trevor interrupted him. "I'm not threatening you. I'm simply stating that we're going to need some help here. I have no doubt that Dad will need to rest and not come into the office for some time. I'm just asking you to come home and help Clayton and me. It won't be forever…just until Dad gets back on his feet."

Wyatt couldn't stand the thought of spending one minute in his father's stuffy office, let alone deal with his brothers on a daily basis. He knew he had to give Trevor an answer but he hesitated before saying exactly what was on his mind.

"Wyatt, at least come home and be with Dad. You owe him that," Trevor implored.

The awkward silence hung between them. Wyatt had no choice but to concede. "Fine. I'll fly out this afternoon."

"Where are you, by the way?" Trevor asked.

"Nantucket. I'm here for the Wine and Food Fest. It just ended, so I won't miss anything in case you were worried."

Wyatt knew that Trevor didn't care one bit whether he was inconvenienced or not, but he still needed to explain that he was almost too busy to come home. Regardless of Trevor's opinion of him, Wyatt did love his brother and the rest of his siblings, even if he failed to show it.

As he liked to think about love, Wyatt's opinion was that there was no use in declaring love for anyone since it most likely wasn't sincere and if it was, would be fleeting at best. He'd never met anyone in his forty years who could challenge his perspective, and so, he'd hold on to his convictions...at least for now.

Wyatt looked at his watch. "I should get into RSW by five o'clock. Make sure there's a car waiting for me. I'll text you when I have more details."

"Thanks, Wyatt," Trevor answered, and then ended the call.

Wyatt threw his cellphone to the side and sat for several minutes trying to imagine what it was going to feel like watching his father unable to respond to him.

The trip south suddenly appealed to him. No matter what his father thought of Wyatt, he no longer had the same power over him that he once did. He had a few things to get off his chest and he vowed to settle things between them once and for all.

What could it hurt? This will be the last time I'll ever set eyes on that man.

It occurred to him that a future without Devon Hutchins in it seemed brighter by the minute.

Jeff Phillips paced the living room floor. He'd just brought his wife Lauren home from the hospital, and while she napped, he looked at the letter from the State Welfare Office.

The home where his brother Peter lived was shutting down, as were several other adult group homes in the state. It meant that Jeff would have to find another similar place for his brother.

With everything else that was going on in their lives, this latest blow was another challenge for his family.

While he waited for word from the police on the fire, Jeff

decided to keep this latest problem from Lauren. He needed her to rest and focus on getting better.

It was true that the fire started in the restaurant, but what wasn't immediately known was why Lauren's real estate business and the other retail businesses never got an alarm from the smoke detectors.

Soon their children would be back home and he wanted everything to appear normal to them. How he and Lauren would accomplish that was anyone's guess. There wasn't much more to do about it than wait for someone to get in touch with Lauren, but that didn't help his anxiety.

Now a stay-at-home dad, Jeff was comfortable in his position and loved that he could be home for their children, however, with the fire and a new baby coming, Jeff wondered if his role would change once more.

He'd grown up in Andover, Massachusetts, and spent his entire life there. He and Lauren met when they were in college and knew immediately that they were going to marry and have a family.

His mother and father had been married for almost thirty years when they divorced. It was difficult on Jeff and his siblings since they all believed their parents to be the perfect example of a good marriage and modeled their own marriages by that example.

The divorce was not his father's idea. His mother wanted a new life, remarried and moved to Connecticut. His father suffered from depression and seemed to give up on life after his ex-wife remarried. He resided in an Assisted Living home near Jeff and Lauren and they visited him often.

Three of Jeff's siblings married and moved away from Andover. All of them, except one, had families of their own and had lives that were far removed from the one they had growing up.

His oldest brother, Peter, however, had Down Syndrome,

lived in an adult group home with three other adult men and seven staff who were like family to Peter. These staff members watched over the residents in shifts.

Since his siblings and parents were unable to care for Peter, the home was the best solution for him. Jeff and Lauren often checked in on Peter and even took him for outings here and there.

Holidays were celebrated at the home, so Lauren and Jeff would stop by just to visit with Peter and made sure he received Christmas and birthday presents every year.

Peter participated in the Special Olympics, beaming as he stood on the podium, receiving his medal in softball. He once even won a huge trophy for Most Inspirational Athlete.

All of that was about to change, and Jeff struggled with how he'd balance it all.

The front door opened and Beth, Gabriel, Christopher and Becca came running inside.

"How's Lauren?" Beth asked.

"She's resting upstairs. She's probably asleep. Did Michael call you all?" Jeff asked.

"Yeah, he explained what happened. I saw some of it on the news which, of course, scared the heck out of us," Christopher answered.

"Does your grandmother know?" Jeff asked.

"Yeah, Michael called her before he called us. He didn't want her to panic if she heard it on the news," Beth said.

"Do they have any idea how the fire started?" Becca asked.

"Well, they've said it definitely started in the restaurant. What they're investigating is why smoke detectors and sprinklers didn't go off," Jeff answered.

"I heard two people died in the fire," Gabriel added.

Jeff nodded. "I heard that. Lauren doesn't know who they are. She thinks it's probably people who were either eating at the restaurant or worked there. The whole thing feels surreal."

"I suppose it's too early to ask what Lauren, Nell and Brian plan to do?" Beth asked.

"What do you mean?" Jeff asked.

"I mean, is she going to find another place for her business or maybe work from home? I mean you can sell houses from anywhere."

Jeff shook his head.

"This isn't the time. The important thing is that Lauren and the baby are going to be fine. Whatever she chooses to do after is up to her. She'll have my full support, even if it means that I have to go back to work outside the house. I can always get my advertising job back."

Jeff didn't have a clue what the future held for his family, but one thing he knew was that they needed income. They had a pretty significant savings, but he didn't want to use that if he could help it. With the baby coming, and Lauren's employment in question, they'd do whatever they could to make ends meet.

CHAPTER 6

Riley Cuthbert stared out the window and sighed, watching the fog envelope everything within view. She'd been up since four o'clock, and as was her usual daily routine, she grabbed a coffee at the local coffee shop and made her way to the Key Lime Garden Inn to prepare breakfast for the guests.

Most mornings Maggie Moretti made scones or quiche while Riley cooked the bacon, eggs, French toast and occasional omelets. But since Maggie was away for a few days, Riley didn't bother trying to make Maggie's scones.

She'd tried a couple of times before to recreate the delicious pastry but she could never quite get them to taste like Maggie's.

Being a chef, Riley understood all too well the reason for it. She knew that it was Maggie's personal touch that made the difference. No chef or cook could dispute the magic that occurs when baking, and in the case of Maggie's scones, magic was the only possible explanation for their incredible flavor.

Iris Bowman, the inn's other cook, came in after breakfast and helped prepare lunch and dinners, but as head chef, it was Riley who ran the kitchen. She was responsible for deciding how best to use the vegetable garden, and worked with Paolo, Maggie's husband, to decide what vegetables and herbs were needed for the day's menus.

The first year that the inn was open, Riley's sister Grace worked in the kitchen until she and her new husband, Connor Hedley, opened the first vegan restaurant on the island. Tropical Vegan was a great success and Riley couldn't be happier for her sister and brother-in-law. However, as much as she loved working with Iris, Riley missed her sister's joking, upbeat and fun ways in the kitchen, and she missed the laughter most of all.

Riley loved her job, but it was the rest of her life that felt out of balance. While everyone around her was falling in love, getting married, having children, or traveling to exotic places in the world, Riley's world centered around her work and her sister's new baby, Penelope.

The inn was quiet and now that Maggie was away in Key West, it was Ciara, Paolo's sister, Millie Brenner, the housekeeper and bookkeeper, and if needed, Sarah, Maggie's daughter, who would run the inn for the next few days.

The season was slowing down and soon the weather would turn hot. Summer weather was always unbearable in Florida but at least the ocean breeze on Captiva Island made the air feel a tad cooler than the rest of the state.

"Good morning, Riley," Millie whispered. "I see none of the guests are up yet?"

Riley shook her head, "Nope. It's just me and my coffee. You should pour a cup."

"Thanks, I think I will."

Riley watched Millie get her coffee and marveled at how the woman had come to the island with no friends, no family, no one in her life, and yet, now, always seemed to be going somewhere or doing something fun when she wasn't working.

"I know it's early morning, but do you mind if I take one of these cookies? They look delicious," Millie asked.

Riley nodded. "Help yourself. I decided to make a new batch of Key Lime Clusters. Let me know what you think."

Riley had been coming up with new cookie recipes lately. She served them to the guests, and then took note which ones got the most positive feedback.

Millie's eyes widened. "Oh my goodness, Riley, these are amazing. I can't stop at just one."

Riley beamed. She'd hoped this batch would impress the guests. Millie's reaction was just the confidence boost she needed.

"I'm thrilled to hear you say that. I hope the guests will feel the same."

"I'm not kidding, Riley. I swear you could make a fortune with your cookie recipes. I had one of your Orange Creamsicle Fingers last week and was disappointed when I came back into the kitchen later and they were all gone."

Riley nodded. "Those were a big hit. I'll make more if you'd like."

"If I'd like? Are you kidding? How about from now on I'll be your new taste tester? You make your cookies and I'll eat a couple from the first batch, you know...just to make sure they're ok so you can serve them to the guests," Millie teased.

Riley laughed. "You've got a deal."

"Between Maggie's scones and your cookies, I'm going to get fat. I've got to get out of here and go to work. I've got tons of entries to do. Besides, it will keep me out of the kitchen and away from your cookies."

Millie started for the office as Riley tried to entice her once more. "Too bad you can still smell the cookies from Maggie's office."

"I'm not listening," Millie joked as she walked out of the room.

Just as soon as Millie left the kitchen, her sister Grace appeared with a small bowl.

"Hey, what are you doing here?" Riley asked.

"Don't you remember that I promised to bring over my new vegan clotted cream? Here is my first batch and if I do say so myself, I think it's delish."

Riley savored a small spoonful, allowing the taste to linger on her tongue.

"Oh my, this is fantastic. You'd never know it wasn't the real thing."

"That's what I said to Connor. I think it will go perfectly with Maggie's scones," Grace replied.

Riley frowned and shook her head. "Bad timing, Gracie. Maggie is out of town for a few days. No scones until she gets back. How long will the cream last?"

Grace shook her head. "It doesn't have to wait for Maggie. You have her recipe, so you make the scones," she insisted.

Riley shrugged. "I've tried, but I can't get them to taste like hers."

Grace grabbed an apron. "Give me the recipe. Let's look it over and try it together. What time does Iris come in?"

"Not until eleven," Riley answered.

"Perfect. We've got plenty of time to make a couple of batches. With the vegan clotted cream, you might have a hit before Maggie gets back."

Riley smiled at her sister. Grace had a new baby and a thriving business, and yet today, as always, she put Riley's needs ahead of her own.

Riley wrapped her arms around Grace and hugged her. "You're the best sister anyone could ever ask for, do you know that?"

Grace hugged her back. "Don't get all sentimental on me. We've got lots of baking to do," she answered.

The sisters baked most of the morning, and for Riley it felt like the old days when she had her sister by her side every day working in the kitchen of the Key Lime Garden Inn.

Riley smiled, thinking that she had started the day feeling

sorry for herself, and yet somehow her sister knew exactly what she was feeling and how to lift her spirits.

While they waited for the scones to bake, they talked about their childhood, how Penelope was growing, and what was new at Tropical Vegan.

When the scones were ready, they let them cool on the counter. After a while they each had a bite of their culinary creation. As Riley closed her eyes and tasted the vegan clotted cream atop the warm scone, she could almost believe they were as good as Maggie's.

"They're not just as good, Riley, they're better. I'm serious. If Maggie was here she'd agree with me."

Riley laughed and hugged her sister. She thanked Grace for her kind and generous lie. Whatever the status of her scones, their time together was what mattered most.

The few precious hours baking alongside her sister was exactly the memory Riley needed to make on this quiet and cloudy Captiva morning.

At the last minute, Chelsea chickened out and decided to call her sister Gretchen instead of showing up on her sisters' doorstep.

"Why did Gretchen say to meet tonight at Blue Heaven?" Maggie asked.

"I'll tell you why," Chelsea answered. "Because she's not telling me the whole truth about their plans down here. The whole time my sisters were visiting Captiva they made it sound like everything was ready for them when they arrived. I'm betting that's not exactly the truth."

"You think they're lying?"

Chelsea shrugged. "I don't want to make the same mistake I made when they were staying with me. I'm going to hold my opinion until I know more."

They arrived at the restaurant at exactly seven o'clock. They walked on the brick walkway leading to a table near a huge Banyan tree.

"I love tables on sand don't you?" Maggie asked Chelsea.

"It's certainly casual, but then again, I think everything in Key West is casual. I love the blue lights."

They stood as soon as Chelsea's sisters, Gretchen, Leah and Tess, approached the table.

"Hey, it's so good to see you two. I can't believe you actually came down here," Tess said.

Chelsea and Maggie hugged the women, and then the waiter interrupted by placing five menus on the table. When they were settled, the waiter took their drink orders.

"This place is very cool," Maggie said. "How did you know about it?"

Gretchen shrugged. "I've actually been down here before. This is Tess and Leah's first time."

"Chelsea, it's not that we're not happy to see you, but the way things were between us when we left Captiva weren't good. It's strange now to see you and Maggie here."

Chelsea nodded. "I get that. When you all left I had to dig deep and look at how I made things difficult for you. I didn't mean to be so negative. I'm not even sure what I was fighting you all about."

Chelsea looked over at Maggie who was smiling. She remembered her friend teasing her about how she wanted to have a front row seat to watch Chelsea apologize, and now the moment had arrived.

"Maggie and I came down to Key West because I needed to tell you all that I'm sorry. I never should have said the things that I did. I also wanted to give you this."

Chelsea took out an envelope from her purse. "It's not as much as Sebastian was going to give you all, but it's something to help you get started."

Leah took the envelope and pulled out a check. "Fifteen thousand dollars?"

Gretchen and Tess looked equally stunned.

"Chelsea, you didn't have to..." Gretchen said before Chelsea interrupted.

"Yes, I did. You all are my family and I want you to succeed with the CoiffeeShop. I know it didn't sound like that's what I wanted, but honestly, I should have made that clear when you all were staying with me. Anyway, let's not make a big fuss about it. You all deserve this money and I'm happy to gift it to you."

The waiter came with their drinks, and Maggie asked that he give them a few more minutes to look over the menu.

"Here's to the success of the CoiffeeShop and your new home on Key West," Chelsea said, raising her glass.

The women clinked their glasses and sipped their tropical drinks, but it was Gretchen who looked less than pleased.

"What is it?" Chelsea asked.

"We all appreciate the money, Chelsea, honest we do. It's just that you should know a few things. First, the building we were hoping to lease has been sold to someone else."

Tess couldn't wait to explain their immediate problem. "Yeah, and the Airbnb that we paid for, isn't really a rental at all. Apparently, someone put this place up for rent without the owner's knowledge. We've been staying at a small motel but it's really disgusting."

Leah nodded. "I swear that someone must have been killed in my room. There's a huge blood stain on the rug...right in the middle of the room."

"None of us are even sleeping under the bedspreads. We sleep on top and Leah won't even take off her hat for fear that bed bugs will start climbing into her hair," Gretchen added.

Maggie kicked Chelsea's leg under the table. "What was that for?"

Maggie ignored her. "You all have to leave that place. You should come stay with us until we get you a better arrangement."

Chelsea looked at Maggie as if her hair was on fire. "What?"

Maggie's piercing stare communicated what she wouldn't say out loud.

"Of course you can stay with us. I mean there is a pull-out queen in the living room and there are two queen beds in the bedroom. I'm sure we'll just squeeze in and make the best of it. Tomorrow we will find you all some place of your own. Provided you all plan to stay and try to make a go of your business plans?"

Tess practically jumped out of her chair. "Oh that's marvelous. Yes, of course we'll stay, but do you think tomorrow we can first spend the day at the beach? It would be so nice just to enjoy a day together without any stress."

Chelsea looked like she was going to throttle her sister, and Maggie caught sight of it, kicking Chelsea once more.

Quickly turning to Maggie, Chelsea yelled, "Ouch. Stop that."

She rubbed her now injured leg and nodded. "Sure, maybe just for the morning, then in the afternoon we look for a place. Deal?"

All three sisters nodded in agreement. "Deal," said Gretchen.

Chelsea didn't know whether to be mad at Maggie or thank her for helping her not ruin the progress she'd made with her sisters.

However, she promised herself that by this time tomorrow, her sisters would have their own place to stay, or she would forget all about making peace with them.

CHAPTER 7

Ciara Moretti couldn't believe she would be married soon. She'd dreamt about her wedding day for about ten minutes when she was a little girl living in Gaeta, Italy. It wasn't that she didn't care about marrying one day, it was mostly because the choice of a husband was out of her control.

From the day she was born, her parents believed they knew best about such matters, and so, it was settled that when Ciara was old enough, she would marry Andrea Mancini, the son of a local fisherman.

To Ciara, dreaming about marrying her Prince Charming was a waste of time, and imagining any other life but one as a fisherman's wife in the town of Gaeta, Italy, would only cause trouble for her. She felt powerless to do anything about it.

She had to admit that when the opportunity arose to leave Italy for America, the stress of her parents' control over her life influenced her decision to go.

Growing up together, Andrea Mancini had become a good friend but in her eyes he was nothing more than that. Andrea felt differently, however. He had fallen in love with Ciara in spite of their parents' involvement. He did his best to talk her out of leaving Italy but it was no use. When Ciara insisted that she would leave Italy and return only for visits now and then, Andrea was just as upset as her parents.

For Ciara, it was an exciting adventure that awaited her and although she couldn't help but feel guilty leaving, it was her brother Paolo who encouraged her. He could see what her future would be and wanted more for his sister. Eventually, he decided to move to the United States to be with her, giving their parents some comfort. They believed that Paolo would represent them and watch over Ciara just as they had for so many years.

Once in America, Ciara was free to make her own decisions about her life. When Paolo came to America to be with her, the adjustment was awkward at first. She pushed back when he tried to impose his opinions about how she should live her life.

Over time, the area of Captiva and Sanibel gave Paolo a life of his own. Both Ciara and Paolo worked hard to become citizens of the United States and took pride in their adopted home. Paolo opened a plant nursery on Sanibel Island and he and Ciara worked to make it a huge success.

After years believing that love would never find its way into her heart and her life, Ciara fell in love with Crawford Powell, a widower who, along with his grown children had welcomed her into their family.

Now that she and Crawford were getting married, she'd somehow agreed to be married on Captiva Island with the reception at the Key Lime Garden Inn. She was grateful to her brother Paolo and sister-in-law Maggie for wanting to host the wedding and without thinking she said yes when they asked her, but it wasn't her first wish.

Crawford was supportive and said that whatever Ciara wanted for her wedding day was fine with him. She was afraid to suggest getting married in Italy given the fact that Crawford had four grown children who would have to adjust their schedules to accommodate her.

Ciara wouldn't push if even one of them couldn't attend. Instead, when he mentioned the possibility of the destination wedding to his children, all four were immediately on board. The day was fast approaching and Ciara had to talk to her brother as soon as possible.

"Ciara, if you put it off any longer, it will be our wedding day," Crawford said. "You have to tell Paolo and Maggie that you want to get married in Italy."

"I know, I know. I was going to but then Maggie went to Key West with Chelsea. I hate having this conversation without her here. My brother will have a fit and Maggie is the only one who can calm him down. I need her in my corner."

"When is she coming home?" Crawford asked.

"Two more days. I promise, just as soon as she arrives I'll go see her and Paolo."

"What about the date?" Crawford asked.

"The plan was for June 3rd but we need more time, Maggie and Chelsea have their lunch-bunch friends coming to Captiva for a bachelorette party on June 10th. It's too much to expect them to go to Italy when they have something big happening as soon as they get back. I can't get married without my brother giving me away, so he and Maggie have to be there."

"I hope Maggie isn't offended. You'll need to make sure that she understands how important getting married in Italy is for you."

"I'm not worried that she will be upset, I'm more concerned that she won't be able to travel to Italy with her busy schedule."

"You realize that the summers can be pretty hot in Italy. When do you think we should go?"

"I think the end of June makes sense, don't you?"

Crawford moved in front of Ciara and wrapped his arms around her. "That works. I'm glad you're not making me wait too long to make you my wife. I can't wait."

As they kissed, Ciara imagined herself standing beside Crawford in the little church overlooking the Gulf of Gaeta and changing her life forever.

Millie looked at the man standing before her and wondered why he wasn't in a hospital bed instead of checking into the Key Lime Garden Inn.

"Welcome, Mr. Benedetti. Have you been to Captiva Island before?"

He nodded. "Many years ago. It's been a long time. Thank you for accommodating my first floor bedroom request."

"Not at all. We're happy that room was available for you. Do you need help with your luggage?"

"No. I'm fine. I'll just go to my room if you don't mind."

Millie smiled. "Of course, it's right over here to your left."

She took the key from the desk and walked slowly past his cane and to his room. She unlocked the door and he followed her inside.

"One of the nice things about this room is that you have your own bathroom. Breakfast is at seven in the morning and we also serve lunch and dinner if you wish. Just fill out the forms on the desk over there and drop them off at the front desk."

"Front desk?" he asked.

"Yes, where we were just a minute ago," she answered.

"Oh, right. Thank you."

"Well, I'll leave you to rest. If there is anything you need please let me know. I'm always around and there is always someone in the kitchen as well. Mr. Moretti is working in the garden at the moment, but you can find him around the property most of the time as well. I hope you'll enjoy your time on the island. We have lots of pamphlets on island activities near the front door if you're interested. "

He nodded. "Thank you."

Millie could sense his desire for solitude. She walked out of his room and closed the door. Walking into the kitchen, she found Riley and Iris working on the dinner menu.

"Did you guys see the man who just checked in?" Millie asked.

"No, why, is he gorgeous?" Riley asked.

Millie smiled. "Not exactly. I mean he was pleasant looking I guess. It wasn't that, it was…I don't know. He just seems different, that's all. He had a large brown paper bag and leaned on a cane. He's probably in his seventies or eighties if I had to guess. I don't think he has any luggage at all."

"No big deal. Everyone knows that Captiva Island is so casual, you could wear your swimsuit and beach cover-up the whole time you're on the island and no one would be the wiser. Is he alone?" Riley asked.

Millie nodded. "Yes, and that's strange as well. We don't often get single people staying here."

She shrugged. "I don't know, I'm sure it's nothing to be concerned about. So, what's on the menu tonight?"

"Paolo just brought in a huge zucchini, so Riley and I are going to make stuffed zucchini and artichokes," Iris answered.

"Sounds wonderful. I may drop by and steal a bite," Millie said. "I've got a little bookkeeping to do, and then I'm heading home. I'll stop in before I go."

Later, when she was done with work and had a bite to eat, Millie walked to the beach before driving home. The beginning of the evening's sunset shone in the sky, and tourists gathered in front of The Mucky Duck to take pictures.

Millie loved her job and Captiva Island, and when she wasn't working, planned to look for a condo nearer to her job. The drive off-island was becoming a bit of a hassle, but beyond that, Millie loved the idea that she would be an islander for the rest of her life.

She crossed her arms over her chest and smiled at the sight.

The crowd was getting larger and there wasn't a cloud in the sky. A young couple stood next to her.

"It's going to be a good one tonight, I can just feel it," the man said.

"I think you're right," Millie answered. "Is this your first Captiva sunset?"

The woman nodded. "It's our honeymoon."

"Oh, my goodness, that's wonderful. Congratulations to you both," she said.

Off to the left and away from the crowd sat Mr. Benedetti, a glass of wine in his hand. Millie watched as he lifted his glass in the air as if to toast the sunset. She couldn't help but feel sad when she watched him, but she was intrigued and plotted to find out more about the man before he went home at the end of the week.

Millie stayed until the sunset was gone, and then walked back to the inn to get her car and drive home. She wondered if she should have said hello to Mr. Benedetti even though he seemed to prefer being alone. Instead, she decided that she'd get to work early the next day before the guests stirred and hoped that he would come into the dining room for breakfast.

She'd have to think of what to say, but one way or the other, Millie needed to find out why a man who seemed so alone in the world would travel to Captiva Island just to sit on the sand and toast a sunset without another person by his side.

CHAPTER 8

The memorial service for Shannon Murphy and Dylan O'Brien took place exactly one week after the fire. Both teenagers, they'd taken jobs at Fire and Wine Pizza and had just graduated high school the week before the tragedy.

Lauren didn't know the victims but felt going to the service was the right thing to do. The entire town of Andover grieved the loss of two young people who had their whole lives ahead of them. Nell, her new husband and Brian sat beside Lauren and Jeff in the church and followed their car to the cemetery.

Lauren still had bandages on her arms and legs and a small one on her face. Several people came up to her to offer condolences as if she was connected to the deceased. In some way, she understood their thinking as she believed everyone who experienced loss in the fire were part of an unspoken club. They all were victims of something that they had no control over. Whether they were injured in the fire or lost their business because of it, their lives were forever changed.

Olivia and Lily were staying at Michael's for the day, and Lauren's grandmother came to help put out a small lunch buffet in the dining room and played host to Lauren's guests.

"I've been to funerals before, but nothing as sad as this one," Jeff said.

Lauren nodded. "I know what you mean. What's really awful is that the whole thing was preventable. Those poor families."

"Did you know that Shannon was the Murphys' only child?" Grandma Sarah asked.

"Yes. It's just awful," Nell added.

"It's a terrible thing to lose a child. I can't even imagine how they must feel," Lauren said.

Everyone except Lauren filled their plates and carried them to the sofa.

Grandma Sarah scolded Lauren.

"Lauren, you have to eat something. If not for you, that baby needs to eat, so get up off that chair and put something in your belly."

Lauren did as her grandmother instructed. As she walked around the table, she looked at Brian.

"You look like you have something on your mind, Brian. I think I can guess what it is. You want to know what happens now?"

Brian shook his head. "No…I, um, well."

Lauren held up her hand. "It's a perfectly good question. The agency went up in flames and now you want to know about your job."

"Yes, of course, but maybe now isn't the time…I…"

Lauren stopped him again. "Now is the time. I've been thinking about it as well." Looking at Nell, she continued, "I don't want either of you to go somewhere else. Phillips Real Estate is still in business. It's just that we don't have a physical office at the moment. Look, we have clients and several of them have called me offering support and their condolences, which I appreciate. What I've found is that they all want to keep working with us. Our business is helping people buy and sell homes. That doesn't change just because our office went up in flames."

She could tell that both Nell and Brian seemed relieved.

"Having said that, if the two of you wish to go somewhere else, I understand. You have to think of your careers," she added.

"Should we look for another location?" Nell asked.

Lauren nodded. "That's exactly what I was thinking. I'm still recovering but it won't be long before I can get back to work."

Jeff interrupted. "Are you sure you want to do that?"

Confused, Lauren looked at him. "What do you mean? The baby isn't due for another four months. I'm not going to sit around here feeling sorry for myself. I've got to get back to work."

Jeff nodded. "I guess we can take comfort in the fact that we didn't own the building. As renters, you can find another office in town."

Nell smiled. "We're not usually in the commercial real estate business, but I'm sure we can find a good match. Brian and I will make it a priority."

Lauren nodded. "Good. I need a few more days before I get out there but you should keep me in the loop. I want to look over everything you find. I'm not sure how much space is available to lease in Andover, but if we have to go to North Andover I'll be fine with that. Try to stay as close to what we've been paying as possible."

Everyone agreed to keep the business running and Lauren was pleased that Brian suggested they talk about her plans. At least now she could focus on getting better. Grateful to have this conversation behind her, Lauren wondered what would become of her insurance claim. Although the building wasn't hers, she still lost equipment and furniture which she'd have to buy again.

She looked at the photos on the living room wall. There, staring back at her, were the most important people in her life. Her two daughters and husband. She cradled her stomach and took a deep breath. In that moment she reminded herself that nothing was more precious than the life she was creating and the home she and Jeff had made. Whatever their future, nothing would ever be more important than that.

Wyatt Hutchins stared at his father and took another sip of his brandy. Since he'd arrived in Florida, the only communication he'd had with his father was an awkward hello from him to his father. Still unable to talk, Devon just stared at his son. Half paralyzed, his father's body language was nonexistent and so there was nothing to indicate that Devon Hutchins was happy to see his son. Wyatt pretended not to care as he kept up the pretense that his father meant nothing to him.

Trevor and Wyatt were not only close as children, but as they grew up found themselves on the same page when it came to the family business. Neither were interested in working for their father as neither of them found the real estate development business exciting.

Where they differed was on the topic of money. Trevor didn't care one bit about being rich, while Wyatt couldn't, and wouldn't, think of anything else.

Trevor went off to help the poor and homeless, giving away everything and anything he ever owned. In Wyatt's mind, Trevor's way of life was abhorrent and he was disgusted by his brother's lack of ambition.

To get his hands on the kind of money and lifestyle he craved, Wyatt had no choice but to first work for his father. To him, his job was not only to learn the real estate business, but to endear him to his father to the point of attaining the role of favorite son.

He told himself that he didn't care for his father's approval, or love. However, Wyatt didn't fool himself on this score. He played the game, he acted the dedicated and loyal son, eventually winning his father's trust, which in Wyatt's mind translated to money and inheritance. But there was still the elephant in the room, the certainty that Devon Hutchins longed for Trevor's admiration.

No matter how hard Wyatt tried to do and be everything his father dreamed a son would be, it was Trevor who won his father's heart time and again.

Trevor could do no wrong in Devon Hutchins' eyes, and so, when Wyatt couldn't stand that reality one minute more, he left town and never looked back. After a week of not showing up for work, his father had no choice but to fire Wyatt and let him go. It would take almost a year before they talked again, and when they did, Wyatt was able to convince his father of his love and devotion, thus ensuring a steady monthly bank deposit from Devon.

Now, sitting in his father's study, sipping his father's brandy, and watching a weak Devon Hutchins slumped in a wheelchair, Wyatt wondered how he could benefit from this new situation.

"Hey, Wyatt," Trevor whispered. "Got a minute? Let's talk in the other room."

Wyatt followed Trevor out onto the lanai where their brother Clayton waited.

"Why do I feel like I'm being set up?" Wyatt asked.

"Nice to see you, too," Clayton answered.

"Look, it's no secret that we've got a situation on our hands. Clayton and I need you to come to work with us. At least until Dad gets better."

Wyatt laughed. "Gets better? Are you kidding? Have you seen him in that wheelchair? Dad is not going to get better."

"Don't say that," Clayton insisted.

Wyatt shook his head and smirked. "Still the lost little boy without his father."

"Put that aside for a moment, will you? We all have issues with Dad. No one is denying that but now's not the time. Talk to your therapist if you have to, but this is about the business and only the business," Trevor said.

"The business *is* Dad," Wyatt yelled. "Open your eyes. You, me and Jacqui are the only ones who couldn't wait to get away from him. Carolyn is just like Mom. They stick their heads in the sand and make their spa appointments and vacations. Carolyn's kids go to the best schools, and heaven help her if the day ever comes when the money stops coming in. Her husband is a joke, and let's not forget Clayton, here, is too afraid of Dad to do anything but say 'yes' and 'please' and 'whatever you say, Daddy.'"

His fists clenched, Clayton moved closer to Wyatt, but did nothing.

"I dare you," Wyatt said, taunting Clayton.

"Stop it!" Trevor yelled and then looked at Wyatt.

"Okay, let's just focus on the money and not the man for a minute. Everyone in this family benefits from the success of this family business…all of us. But the money will stop flowing from the business to your way of life if it goes under. I'll grant you this…you're right, the business is Dad, and we're going to have to do some juggling in light of his illness. If word on the street is that he's done for, it will have a negative impact on all of us. Maybe not forever, but in the short term. So, if you want to keep living in the manner to which you've become accustomed, at least for the foreseeable future, we all need to pull together… including you."

Wyatt hated to admit that Trevor was right. If he wanted to keep the status quo, he'd have to do whatever he could to keep the business running and profitable.

He finished the rest of his brandy and put the glass down on a bar cart.

He looked at Clayton and then Trevor.

"Fine. I'll stay and help but I can't commit to a specific date when I'll want to leave. All I can promise is a couple of months at a time, or, if there is a miracle and Dad is well enough to return to work. Is that good enough for the two of you?"

Trevor nodded. "Yeah, it'll do."

"Fine with me," Clayton added.

Wyatt looked around the lanai. "I'll stay here as long as I can stand it. If it gets too awful, I'll need to stay somewhere else."

Wyatt couldn't yet figure out the value of living so close to his parents. The only thing he knew was that the house was big enough to keep them from running into each other, and that would have to do for now.

CHAPTER 9

"This is the fifth place we've looked at this morning. If my sisters don't pick one of these houses, I'm going to kill them," Chelsea whispered.

Doing her best to calm Chelsea down, Maggie said, "Listen, I know you're about to lose your mind, but remember why we came here. You wanted to put your differences aside and move forward. The last thing you want to do is start another dispute."

"We've made our decision," Gretchen said. "We're going with the first place."

"I just love that kitchen," Tess said.

"I'm so excited that I'm finally going to have a pool. Do you know how many years I fussed at David to put in a pool?"

"Well, now you have your very own," Chelsea said.

"The real estate agent is helping us find the right commercial property too. I'm glad because she was so wonderful to work with helping us find this place. She already has two places she wants us to see," Leah announced.

Chelsea nodded. "That is great news, however, you ladies will have to check those places out on your own. Maggie and I have to head back to Captiva."

Gretchen wrapped her arms around Chelsea. "Thank you so much for coming to visit Chelsea, it means the world to us." She looked at Maggie and reached for her hand. "You too, Maggie."

"Yes, it's been so wonderful to have you both here. I'm sorry to see you go. Can you imagine the fun we'd have if we all lived down here together?" Tess asked.

Maggie couldn't imagine such a thing knowing that Chelsea would lose her mind living that close to them.

Chelsea shook her head. "I can't, actually."

Everyone laughed and headed for lunch before Maggie and Chelsea packed their bags to leave early that afternoon. When they were finally on the road, Maggie looked out the window at the water and colorful buildings.

Chelsea tapped her shoulder.

"So, are you going to tell me what's been bugging you this morning, or am I going to have to wait until we're back in Captiva? You might as well spit it out because you and I both know I can't wait that long."

"I don't know Chelsea, but I feel something isn't right with Lauren. Michael said that she's fine and getting better all the time, but I can't help feeling anxious about her. She and I have always been able to sense the other's feelings and worries. You should have seen how overprotective I was of her when she was a baby."

"Really, Maggie? I would never have guessed," Chelsea teased.

Maggie smiled and rolled her eyes, "I have no doubt you think that I'm like that with all my kids, but it's different with Lauren. She was my first girl. "

"She is a lot like you," Chelsea said.

"I kept thinking about what lessons I was teaching her. At one point, I was convinced that because Daniel was unfaithful, that somehow Lauren saw our marriage in such a negative light, that she'd never pick the right guy to marry when she got older."

"Maggie, you and Daniel had a lot of loving examples of how

to be with each other. Sure there were times later in life when people started seeing what he was up to but for years most people were jealous of your seemingly perfect family."

Maggie wasn't convinced.

"You've been a great mother and I think that's what you should remember," Chelsea added.

Maggie shrugged. "Well, thank heaven that she and Jeff do have a good marriage and are creating a beautiful family of their own. I know that Lauren wasn't burned in the fire, but there are other, more long-lasting injuries that could harm her and the baby."

"What are you saying?"

"My family has already dealt with Post Traumatic Stress too many times. First with Daniel dying, then with Christopher when he lost his leg, and then Michael when he was shot. I feel like I can almost anticipate it happening to Lauren."

"What do you want to do about it? Do you want to fly to Boston and be with her?"

Maggie shrugged. "I don't know. She might think I'm overreacting, and Jeff might feel like he needs to handle it. I think the only thing I can do is wait for her to…"

Chelsea smiled. "Need her mother?"

Maggie laughed. "You know me too well, Chelsea Marsden."

Lauren had already signed the lease to the new office space when Jeff walked into the house carrying three grocery bags.

"I've got a couple more in the trunk. I forgot to eat before I went shopping. What've you got there?"

Lauren held several papers up. "It's the lease on my new place. I'm back in business."

Jeff put the bags down on the kitchen island and then took the papers from Lauren. He read the document and then looked at her. "Don't you think you're moving too fast on this? I thought you'd take more time to heal and rest."

Dismissing his concerns, she walked into the kitchen and started pulling the groceries out of the bags.

"What's for dinner tonight? I don't mind telling you that I've been happy not to do any of the cooking ever since we swapped roles last year. If I haven't told you before, you're a really good cook," she said.

He walked over to her and took her hand in his. "Lauren, you're not listening. It's too soon for you to go back to work. Give it another week or two."

Lauren tilted her head as if she didn't understand.

"Another week or two? Are you crazy? Imagine what people would think if I did that. They'd assume I was out of business and would go somewhere else, and you know what that would mean? Once they've connected with another agency, they'd probably stay with them. Not to mention that Nell and Brian might go somewhere else. No, I can't take that risk. I won't."

"Lauren, you know that Nell and Brian are loyal to you and would never leave. That's just an excuse."

Lauren turned to Jeff and looked him in the eye. "I'm not talking about this again. It's *my* business and *my* decision to make, and I've made it."

She stormed out of the room and left him standing in the kitchen. Mixed emotions overwhelmed him. Grateful when Olivia and Lily distracted him laughing at something on the television.

He continued to put the groceries away, pushing his building anger aside. He'd deal with his feelings and concerns later that night after he'd put the girls to bed.

Jeff knew it would be a long, sleepless night trying to figure out how best he could help his wife, and not take her disrespectful behavior personally. Whether he could do that remained to be seen.

Mr. Benedetti didn't come down for breakfast the first two days of his stay. On the third day he walked the perimeter of the Key Lime Garden Inn's grounds, leaning on his cane. He met Paolo in the garden right after he'd had his lunch.

"So, you're Italian?" he asked Paolo.

"Yes. I was born in Italy but I've lived here for many years now. How are you today, Mr. Benedetti?"

"Please, call me Matteo," he answered.

"All right. I hope you're enjoying your stay on the island."

"Yes, Captiva is a special place, indeed. You know, my father was Italian. He was born in the U.S. He's gone now. My mother was English, a fact that my father kept from his family when he returned from the war as a married man."

Paolo was intrigued. "I'm sorry, I don't understand. How could your father keep that information from his family? Surely, they would find out when they met your mother."

Mr. Benedetti nodded. "Yes, you're right. However, my father didn't return to the United States with my mother. He came home without her. He left her back in Pershore, England. She didn't come to this country until almost a year later."

Paolo was amused by this story and wanted to know more.

"How about you and I have something to drink? We can sit near the pond and you can tell me about your parents."

Mr. Benedetti seemed pleased that Paolo had suggested they spend time together. "I'd like that."

"What would you like? We have iced tea, lemonade..."

With a twinkle in his eye, Mr. Benedetti looked around the property and then back at Paolo and whispered, "Do you have any wine?"

Paolo smiled. "I'm sure I can find some. Why don't you go sit by the pond and I'll bring us two glasses?"

Matteo Benedetti nodded and Paolo, excited to have another

man to talk to, ran to get the wine. When he returned, his new friend was talking to the koi fish.

"You like fish?" Paolo asked.

"I do. I used to go fishing all the time, but…"

Matteo seemed to drift off without concern that he hadn't finished his thought. He raised his glass. "Salute."

"Salute," Paolo responded, and then joined Matteo on the bench. "So, tell me, what was your father doing in America all the while knowing that he had a wife back in England?"

"Working, of course. He needed to make a living after all. Everyone thought there was something strange about his behavior though. My father was a very handsome man and all the girls liked him. Before he went to the war he must have been dating one girl after the other. He played the field and never thought about getting married. He used to say 'When I met your mother, that was it for me. I never looked at another woman.'"

"What did your family say when your father finally told them?" Paolo asked.

"Well, as you can imagine, they weren't very happy. But, all that changed when my mother came to America to live. My grandmother was tough and not easy to please, but my grandfather liked her immediately," he said.

"That's a great story," Paolo said. "What about you?"

"What do you mean?"

"I mean, did you ever get married yourself?"

Matteo nodded. "I did. I was fortunate to marry my best friend. Louise and I were married for forty-six years before she died."

"I'm so sorry," Paolo responded.

A deep sadness came over Matteo's face and Paolo wanted to say something comforting; instead, the two men sat in silence for several minutes drinking their wine.

After he was done with his wine, Matteo got up from the bench and handed Paolo his empty glass.

"Well, I best be on my way. Have a good day, Paolo, and thanks for the wine."

Paolo watched as Matteo limped back to the inn.

Matteo didn't leave the inn until it was near sunset. As the sky turned orange and pink, Matteo Benedetti walked toward the ocean, a bag in one hand, his cane in the other, and a small beach chair on his back.

CHAPTER 10

Riley, Iris and Millie gathered around the kitchen island and asked Maggie one question after another about Key West and whether it was anything like Captiva.

"Now that I've been there, I can officially report that Key West is nothing like Captiva. It's a great place and lots of fun, but it has a more party-like atmosphere."

Maggie looked at Riley and Iris. "I think the two of you should go there. I think it has a younger person vibe, but what do I know?"

"One of these days, I'm going to drag Riley there," Iris said. "We'll get Grace and her husband to be backup and then we're off. What do you say Riley?"

Riley shrugged. "Sure, sounds good to me."

Maggie wasn't home for more than an hour before Ciara came knocking on the back door. Paolo followed behind her.

"Welcome home. Did you and Chelsea have a good time?"

Maggie hugged Ciara. "We did. We had to squeeze in the fun in between Chelsea dealing with her sisters' real estate issues, but overall it was great." She looked at each of the women and asked the question she was afraid to ask. "How have things been around here? Any disasters?"

"Everything was great. It's a little slow so except for one couple and one single man in the downstairs bedroom, it's been pretty quiet," Millie answered.

"Oh? One single man? Can I assume he's one handsome, single man?" Maggie asked.

"He's single, all right. If I had to guess, I'd say he's in his late seventies. He's a widower and not even remotely looking for a girlfriend."

Confused, Maggie said, "That seems odd, doesn't it?"

Paolo shrugged, went to the refrigerator and pulled out a cannoli. "Which part? That he's single or doesn't want a girlfriend."

Maggie rolled her eyes, "No, silly. That he's here on Captiva by himself. I don't think we've ever had an elderly, single man alone here before."

Paolo leaned into his wife and winked. "I'd be careful when you say elderly, my love. We're not that far behind."

"Oh, for heaven's sake, I'm not focused on the number, I want to know why he's here."

"You don't think he just wanted a vacation?" Millie asked.

Maggie shook her head. "No, I don't. There's another reason, I'm sure."

Paolo looked squarely in his wife's eyes. "It doesn't matter because it's none of our business, right? Leave the man alone. If he wants to talk, he will. If not, let him be on his way."

Maggie pretended to heed Paolo's warning, but secretly, she had already started to devise a way to find out more about her guest.

Ciara interrupted the talk about Mr. Benedetti and directed the conversation to her upcoming wedding.

"Maggie, Paolo, can the three of us go over to the carriage

house and talk about the wedding? Crawford should be here any minute to join us."

Maggie was exhausted and had visions of soaking in a hot bathtub under a pile of bubbles. However, Ciara looked anxious and with Crawford joining them, there was little she could do but agree. "Of course, let's go now because I see a nap in my future," she answered.

Crawford showed up just as they were crossing the driveway.

"Hey, honey, great timing," Ciara said as she grabbed his hand.

"Hey, Paolo, Maggie. How was your trip to Key West?"

"Enjoyable but I have to tell you, I love Captiva so much that when I leave the island I feel like I've left my vacation instead of going on one."

"I understand completely. It's one of the perks of working and living in a place that the world comes to for vacation. We're all very blessed to live here."

"Does anyone want something to drink?" Paolo asked.

"Nothing for me, " Crawford answered. "Ciara?"

She shook her head. "No, thank you."

"So, I guess I should probably get a pad of paper to write down ideas for the wedding. Let me go get..."

"Wait, Maggie, you don't have to write anything down." She looked at Crawford for support, and then took a deep breath. "First, we want to thank you so much for offering to have the wedding here at the inn. We know you'd do a fantastic job, it's just that... well, Crawford and I talked and we agreed that it would be wonderful to have the wedding in Gaeta, Italy, instead."

Maggie noticed that Ciara wasn't making eye contact with Paolo. She assumed it was because she thought he'd be angry, but that wasn't what happened. Instead, he came to her and pulled her into an embrace.

"Ciara, this is wonderful news. A long time ago, I worried that when the time came for you to marry, that you wouldn't want to go back home to Gaeta for the ceremony. I know our parents are gone, but our homeland is still important to both of us. I'm so very proud of you for making this decision."

Ciara wept as her brother held her close. "I thought you'd be upset with me. I mean, you and Maggie have to be there. You have to give me away."

Maggie panicked. "Wait. I have my lunch-bunch friends coming the week after your wedding. There is so much to do to get ready, I thought that I'd at least have the week to prepare."

Ciara turned to Maggie. "Oh, we've decided to change the wedding date until the end of June. Both Finn and Becca wouldn't be able to get the time off until then, so we moved the date. This way, you and Paolo can come after your friends' visit. How does that sound?"

Maggie clapped her hands together. "That's perfect. This will work out for everyone. Now, you must tell me, what can I do to help with the wedding? Even though it's in Italy, you're still going to need help with some things. The guys don't care about this stuff, so, why don't you, Sarah and I sit down and make some plans. We're going to need to go shopping for your dress and for hers."

Suddenly, Maggie wasn't tired at all. The thought of an Italian wedding and another trip to Italy stirred whatever adrenaline she had in her body. With June fast approaching she took note of all the things she needed to do.

Her friends would arrive in two weeks. Her mother, in ten days, and a family trip to Italy at the end of the month meant her plan to adopt a puppy would have to be put off until July.

Maggie's full calendar should have excited her, however, the nagging feeling that her daughter was struggling dampened her spirits. Nothing was more important than her children's happiness, and anything that got in the way of that would need to be taken off her calendar…even an Italian wedding.

Millie waited in the office until she heard the first floor bedroom door open and shut. It was eight-thirty in the morning and Mr. Benedetti was awake and out of his room. However, he didn't come to the dining room for breakfast, instead, he walked out the front door of the Key Lime Garden Inn.

She ran to the front bay window and watched him limping down the driveway and out onto the street. Her work would have to wait. Millie wanted to know where the inn's mysterious guest was going, and the only way she could find out was to follow him.

She stayed as far away as possible so he couldn't see her. When he walked as far away as the corner variety store at the corner of Andy Rosse Lane, a taxi pulled up alongside him, and he got inside.

Frustrated, Millie turned to walk back to the Key Lime Garden Inn and her housekeeping duties. She was in the laundry room when Riley called her into the kitchen.

"Hey Riley, what's up?"

"Hi, Millie. I was wondering if you wouldn't mind driving up to Jerry's to get a few things. Here's a list and money. That should cover it. I'd go myself, but Iris isn't coming in today and I've got so much to do to prepare for tonight's dinner. I need this stuff as soon as you can get there.

"No problem. I wish I knew about this earlier though. I could have followed Mr. Benedetti."

"What do you mean?" Riley asked.

Millie didn't want anyone to hear, so she kept her voice low and quiet. "I'm trying to find out more about him. He limped all the way to The Island Store and then got into a taxi."

"So?"

"So, why didn't he have the taxi pick him up here? What is he trying to hide?" Millie answered with more than a bit of suspicion in her voice.

Riley laughed. "I'm sure he's not trying to hide anything. He probably wanted to walk a little first. I'm not sure why he's using a cane, but maybe it's only temporary and he wants to get some exercise."

Millie wasn't convinced. "That's a stretch, Riley. He can get his exercise just walking around here, he doesn't need to go all the way to Andy Rosse. I think he doesn't want us to know where he goes every day."

Riley leaned over the kitchen island. "And, so you've decided not to respect his wishes? Leave the man alone. If anything, he seems lonely to me."

Millie shook her head. "I know lonely, Riley. He's not lonely. He's on a mission. I'm certain that he came to Captiva for a reason other than to relax and have a vacation."

Riley shrugged. "Okay, but it's your funeral. If Maggie or Paolo hear about this, I don't think they'll be so happy to know you're bothering their guest."

"Don't be silly. I'm not bothering Mr. Benedetti one bit."

"Well, for now, all I need is for you to forget about him and do this one errand for me. You can play snoop on your own time but try not to let the man know what you're doing. The last thing we need is to get a negative review online."

Riley went back to her cooking and Millie took the list and money for the market. As she drove to Sanibel, Millie thought more about what Riley advised and couldn't ignore the potential problems if she continued to stalk Mr. Benedetti.

Millie had overcome so much in the last year, and she treasured the relationship she had with the Morettis. She didn't want to risk losing the faith they had in her. And so, although still intrigued by the man, she would have to gain his trust for him to freely share any information with her.

She couldn't explain, not even to herself, why it mattered so much to know more about him, but there was something about the way he carried himself and her absolute conviction that something plagued his every move.

Whatever his worries, she'd be content to sit quietly and listen to his stories, and hope that she'd be able to lift his spirits and soothe his pain even if it was short-lived.

CHAPTER 11

"I just got off the phone with Beth," Sarah said.

"Oh? How is she doing?" Maggie asked.

"She's worried about Lauren and so am I."

"Why? What's happened?"

Sarah shook her head. "Nothing really. Beth says she has a weird feeling that Lauren isn't really facing what happened to her in the fire."

"What does Jeff say?" Maggie asked.

"I don't think she's talked to him since it happened. It's just her gut feeling and you know Beth. She's usually right."

Maggie's stomach turned at the thought of her daughter suffering in silence. It was just the way Maggie used to deal with troubles she didn't want to face. She'd been holding back and not trying to interfere but by now, with no call from Lauren, Maggie knew instinctively that Beth was right.

"Mom, I've got other news. Devon's had a stroke. I was going to call you but you were away and we've been so crazy at our house. On top of everything Noah's been sick."

"Oh, Sarah, I'm so sorry to hear this. Is he going to be okay? How bad is it?"

"It's pretty bad. I guess Eliza found him on the floor of their bedroom. She's understandably frantic."

"I can imagine. What's this about Noah?"

Sarah smiled, "This time it's just a little cold but you know how much I worry about him."

"I know that feeling only too well," Maggie answered.

"I guess Devon's stroke will have a big impact on the family business. Trevor is even trying to get his brother Wyatt to come into the firm in the interim. I hope he does come back. Not only for the sake of the business, but it would be nice to take some of the workload from Trevor. Maybe I'll even see him more," she said.

"Isn't Wyatt the brother who parties all the time and travels around the globe with gorgeous women? He's rather infamous from what Trevor says."

Sarah nodded. "That's the one. He's going to have to change his ways if he comes back home."

"What is Trevor's plan for when Devon returns?" Maggie asked.

"Nothing short of reconciliation will make Trevor happy, and he thinks it will make Devon proud. I just hope he's not setting himself up for a huge disappointment. I agree the family would benefit from everyone getting along, but I'm not so sure at what cost, and neither does Trevor. I guess we'll just have to wait and see."

"Let me get my notebook before we head over to Chelsea's. I'll be right back."

Still thinking about Lauren, Maggie walked into her office, picked up her notebook and then looked at her calendar and sighed. With so much to do in the next two weeks, it was impossible to squeeze in a trip to Boston, but the urge was strong to see

Lauren. She'd wait a little longer and if she didn't hear from Lauren, she'd make the call herself.

Chelsea came in through the front door carrying a briefcase. "Are you guys ready? I had to stop at the bank and then the craft store. I was running low on paint supplies. I've got my car so you don't have to walk."

"Almost. Sarah and I were just talking about Lauren. Are we late?" Maggie asked.

"No. I just thought I'd stop here first."

Maggie was certain that Jane's bachelorette party would be a big success. She hoped that today's meeting would give her a better idea of what Jane wanted for the event. Her lunch-bunch friends did their best to help Jane with planning her wedding from up north, but it was left to Maggie to organize the details of the bachelorette party on Captiva.

When Maggie and Chelsea walked into the kitchen it struck Maggie that Sarah hadn't said a word about Ciara's wedding. "Have you talked to Ciara about her wedding plans?"

Sarah shook her head, "Not lately. As I said, even if she did try to call me, I probably never noticed a message. She did say that she wanted to go shopping with me to find a dress for her and for me. I realize it's last minute but…"

"You better sit down for this news. She wants to get married in Italy and it won't be until the end of June now."

"What? Italy? I can't go to Italy," Sarah lamented.

"Well, honey, to be fair I don't think she knows about Devon. You'll just have to explain that things are a bit up in the air right now."

"I feel horrible. I'm her Maid of Honor."

"I know, sweetie. I'm sure she'll understand."

Sarah slumped on the nearest chair. "You don't understand. I've always wanted to go to Italy. With everything that Trevor is dealing with, I know he'll say that it's impossible right now. What bad timing."

Maggie watched as her daughter pouted for a few minutes before composing herself for the afternoon meeting.

"Well, I guess we should focus on one thing at a time. I'm disappointed but the situation can't be helped. I'll call Ciara later. So, this is what I'm thinking. Jane should have a sash around her that reads 'Bride' and maybe even a princess crown. Do your friends like karaoke?"

"Sarah, I appreciate those suggestions, but everything you mentioned feels more appropriate for younger women. We're all in our late fifties, well, except for Rachel who is younger, but even she wouldn't want to get up on stage to sing."

"Oh, Mom, don't be such a stick in the mud. Age is just a number and let's not forget that with Chelsea as the ring-leader, you all have managed to get into some wild situations in the past."

"Shhh. I don't want Riley and Iris to hear you," Maggie whispered.

"Too late," Riley said.

"Well, that was a while ago. Things are different now and we'd like to have fun but not get arrested," Maggie answered.

"Did you really get arrested?" Iris asked.

"Chelsea did. I was able to escape just in time."

"Thank heaven she did too because I needed her to bail me out. It was a misunderstanding anyway. All I did was remove a statue from a fountain that was broken. I was going to fix it and bring it back, but instead the owner of the bar called the cops on me. It was so ridiculous."

Maggie rolled her eyes. "I didn't have to bail you out. I convinced the guy not to press charges."

Sarah, Riley and Iris laughed as Millie came in carrying a bunch of towels for the laundry. "What's so funny?"

"Oh, we were talking about how Chelsea and Mom were out partying and almost got thrown in jail."

Maggie shook her head. "Don't listen to them, Millie. It's a huge exaggeration if you ask me. Anyway, we're headed over to Chelsea's house for the afternoon. We've got bachelorette party planning, and then a lunch-bunch Zoom meeting."

"Oh, Sarah, that reminds me," Riley said. "Ciara told me to tell you that she'll call you tonight about finding a day when the two of you can go shopping for wedding stuff."

Sarah rolled her eyes. "Perfect timing. What am I going to do? I appreciate that Ciara is letting me pick whatever I want to wear for a Maid of Honor dress, but now that the wedding is in Italy, I might have to tell her I can't be her Maid of Honor after all."

"Let's not worry about that right now. Let's head over to Chelsea's and then you and Ciara can talk later. If anybody needs me, just call my cell," Maggie said. "I'll be back around dinnertime."

"Have fun," Millie said.

The lunch-bunch ladies had been Chelsea and Maggie's book club friends back when they all lived in Massachusetts. The book club had twelve members, but it was Diana, Kelly, Jane, Rachel, Chelsea and Maggie who decided to leave the club and form their own.

It wasn't because they didn't want to read books and talk about them, it was because they had found themselves wanting to talk about other things.

They'd always said they'd go back, but when Chelsea and her husband moved to Captiva Island, Rachel moved back home to Cape Cod and became part owner of a vineyard, and then Jane's job had her traveling the globe, the once-a-month lunch-bunch get-togethers, sometimes even on video, made the most sense.

Over the years, the women formed the kind of bond that distance and time couldn't break. They each had major life challenges and through each one, the group would stay in touch and support one another. They were able to share happy times as well, and with Jane getting married, a bachelorette party on Captiva was the perfect way to see each other once again after so many months apart.

Maggie was so happy to see her friends again. "I miss you guys," she said.

"We miss you all too," said Kelly. "I'm really excited about the bachelorette party though. Just seeing everyone in person again makes me ecstatic."

"So, everyone, I asked my daughter Sarah to join us so she can help us plan."

Sarah waved into the camera. "Hi. Nice to see everyone."

"Hey, Sarah. How's your family? I understand you have three now?" Diana asked.

"Yup, three little ones under the age of seven. It's fun and chaotic all at the same time."

"I bet," said Kelly.

"How about we get this meeting started?" Chelsea added. "I'd like to add my two cents to the party idea. I don't know about you ladies, but I am totally in for a spa day."

"Oh, I like that idea," Maggie said.

"Me too. I want the works…nails, toes, massage, facial, sauna…what do you say, ladies?" Jane asked.

"I think that's a great idea. Since you all are staying for a week, why don't you do a few things? One day can be a spa day, another you can charter a boat, another day you all can bar hop or, more likely, restaurant hop with appetizers in one place, a meal at another and dessert and coffee or after dinner drinks somewhere else. Then, maybe one night, you invite me, Riley, Iris and Ciara to join you for a night out dancing. I know Mom and Chelsea know of a few places that are perfect for dancing."

Sarah winked at her mother, and smiled when she kicked her leg under the table.

"I love it," Jane answered. "What does everyone else think?"

"I'm in," said Rachel. "We've produced some amazing wines, but my body has been put through a lot to make it happen. I don't remember the last time I was in a spa."

"Great," Sarah said. "I can make all the arrangements and will give Mom the information so you'll be good to go when you arrive. Do you have a car?"

"Yes, I've rented a van so we all can pile in. I think it has enough room for eight people," Chelsea said.

"Perfect. I think you ladies will have so much fun," Sarah said.

"Considering the last time we were together on Captiva I missed out on some of the fun, I think this time will be a blast," Rachel said.

"Well, that's what happens when you go into labor on a boat out in the middle of the Gulf. We were lucky you didn't have your baby right there," Maggie added.

"I'll say. It would have been a sight to see for sure. I don't think any of us ever delivered a baby before," Chelsea said.

"Well, I think we've got a plan. Anyone have anything else to add?" Sarah asked.

"No, I think we're good. I can't wait to see everyone," Jane said. "And thank you all for doing this. I just couldn't see myself getting married without celebrating with my best friends. It means the world to me."

Sarah excused herself to another room when Ciara arrived, and the women spent the rest of their time together drinking wine and talking about Jane's wedding. Ciara and Sarah were doing the same on the lanai, and soon, when the lunch-bunch ladies were done, Maggie and Chelsea would join them.

Sarah shared the latest developments within her family and Ciara asked her to wait another week before she made any permanent decision. In the meantime, Ciara wanted Sarah to go shopping with her just in case Sarah did make it to Italy.

For the better part of the afternoon Chelsea's house had become wedding central and the excitement was palpable. The only thing that worried Maggie was the look on Diana's face when they talked about falling in love, romance, the perfect man, and the blessing of long-lasting marriages.

Maggie couldn't be certain but her gut was usually right about such things. If something was wrong in Diana's marriage, Maggie and the others would soon hear about it. To Maggie, that was the gem in their friendship, knowing that whatever lay ahead in each of their lives, the women would take the journey together.

CHAPTER 12

"I'm going to need another week or two. My business isn't done and I'm not exactly sure how much time I need on Captiva. Is it possible that you have a room available? I don't mind if it's on the second floor. I can make do if you can accommodate me," Matteo said.

Millie scratched her head. "Well, I know that Mrs. Moretti has a rather large function coming up here at the inn. She's not here at the moment, but I can check with her to see what's available."

"I'd appreciate it. I'll be sitting at the gazebo for a spell, and then I plan to have dinner in the dining room. If you don't see me at either location I'll be in my room. Please let me know just as soon as you can."

Millie nodded. "Of course."

Matteo walked through the kitchen, waved at Riley and went out the back door.

Millie looked over the registration book and sighed. Other than Mr. Benedetti, there were two couples staying at the inn but they were scheduled to check out in two days.

Nothing was scheduled for the remainder of the month. Since

June, July and August were slower than the rest of the year, that wasn't unusual.

Maggie arrived just before dinner.

"Mr. Benedetti would like to stay longer. He's not certain how many days he needs but he said that his business wasn't finished and he needed to stay on Captiva a while longer."

"How much longer?" Maggie asked.

"He says a week or two."

"Oh my. That could be a problem. I've got my friends coming to stay for a week, and we've got several things planned. I was hoping not to book anyone for the rest of June."

Millie nodded. "I know, but..."

"But, you like the man and want him to stay?"

"Is it that obvious? It's not what you think though."

Millie looked around to make sure no one heard her.

"I don't have a romantic interest in Mr. Benedetti. I'm just curious about him. I mean, he seems rather mysterious, don't you think?" she whispered.

"Funny you should say that. To be honest, I'm dying to know what's up with him. I mean, he arrived with just one paper bag. He's got probably two or three pairs of pants and shirts. He does have a backpack and I've noticed a large leather crossbody bag that I think is a briefcase."

"Well, if he stays will it really impact your event? He keeps to himself. He doesn't make any noise. Besides, maybe your friends could help us solve this mystery?"

Maggie shook her head. "No. I don't want them involved with this at all. They're here to have a good time and the last thing I want is for Mr. Benedetti to have a bunch of women interrogating him. Let me think for a minute."

"He's out at the gazebo and he's going to have dinner here. He asked that we let him know just as soon as possible."

"I'll go out and talk to him. Thanks, Millie."

Maggie found Matteo sitting under the gazebo with a cup of tea.

"Good afternoon, Mr. Benedetti."

"Please call me Matteo. I had a nice conversation with your husband the other day. You have a lovely place here."

"Thank you. May I join you for a bit?"

"Of course," he answered, trying to get up to be polite.

"No, please, sit. Millie tells me that you'd like to stay with us a bit longer. I just wanted to let you know that since I have a reunion event here at the inn, there might be lots of people and activity that you might not appreciate. I can let you keep the first floor room, but it could get noisy," she explained.

"Oh, that's fine. I'll be happy for the company," he said.

Maggie was surprised by his response. She was convinced that he wanted to be left alone.

"You will? I'm surprised to hear that."

He smiled. "I guess I can understand why you'd think that. After all, I haven't been much of a social butterfly now have I?"

"I'm sorry, I didn't mean to imply or pass judgment. Most people don't like noise when they're staying at a Bed & Breakfast."

He looked off at the horizon and hesitated before responding. "Captiva has a special place in my heart. It's not all happy memories, but they are *my* memories and significant in my life. I just need more time to…truly appreciate the island."

He gave away nothing with his words, and Maggie was more confused and intrigued than ever.

"I don't want to pry, but I do want to offer my patient and empathetic ear. I'm a good listener, so any time you wish to talk, I'm here."

He smiled and nodded. "Thank you, and I'm sorry that I can't give you a specific date for when I'll be checking out of your home. I will let you know just as soon as I can."

Maggie nodded. "That's good enough for me. The Key Lime

Garden Inn is more than a Bed & Breakfast for our guests. I like to think of it as a home away from home. For the time that you'll be with us, this is your home."

"Thank you. That's exactly how I'll think of it."

"I'll leave you to your tea. I believe dinner will be ready in about thirty minutes. You have a pleasant evening, Mr.…Matteo. If you'd like to truly appreciate the inn at dusk, some time on the porch swing listening to the windchimes is a good way to end the day."

Maggie walked back to the inn and wondered if Matteo would sit on the swing or walk to the ocean and once again watch the sunset as he'd been doing most nights. Either way she was convinced that he'd spend the time in quiet contemplation and would hopefully consider sharing his thoughts with her when he was ready.

Trevor did a double-take when he walked past his father's office. Smoking a cigar with his feet up on the desk was his brother Wyatt. A grin formed when he saw Trevor standing in the doorway.

"Good morning, brother. You're a bit late getting to work this morning, aren't you?" Wyatt asked.

"Did you have a hard time finding your office? I told Janet at reception to take you there. What happened?"

"It's too small. I like this one better."

"I take it you also like Dad's cigars or did you bring your own?"

Wyatt sat up straight, his feet on the floor. "Listen, if you want me to work here, then you're going to have to get used to me sitting at Dad's desk. I don't need the employees thinking that I'm some mail clerk. We've got to keep up appearances, not to mention morale."

"This has nothing to do with morale and everything to do with optics. You want everyone to think that you're in charge."

Wyatt took a long puff on the cigar and smiled. "Well, I *am* the first-born son."

Clayton joined Trevor at the door. "Well…are you going in or are you going to stand here holding up the door?"

They walked into the office and sat on the sofa. "So, this is your office now?" Clayton asked.

"I'm tired of talking about this. I don't care where you sit. Let's get to work," Trevor announced. "Wyatt, I need you and Clayton to meet me and the architect in Tampa to look over the new development site. I've got to give them the go-ahead to break ground but I need one last meeting with the architect, and we all should be there. Dad had planned this meeting and the three of us were scheduled, so you'll need to go in his place."

"When is it?"

"Thursday morning at nine."

Wyatt shook his head. "No can do. I've got tee time at 8:30. We'll have to reschedule."

Trevor instinctively knew his brother was trying to provoke him, but he wasn't going to let him control the room.

"So, Wyatt, here is how this is going to go. You'll either work with Clayton and me to continue to build this company and make it a success, or you can go play golf or anything else you'd like. But, let me be clear so there is no misunderstanding. I'm not Dad. I'm not going to enable you for the rest of your life."

Wyatt rolled his eyes as if he anticipated a lecture.

"I hope with all my heart that Dad gets better and comes back to work, but at some point he will die. The three of us can run this place and you can go play golf every chance you get. You can spend money like it grows on trees for all I care. But, if you refuse to work for it, I will make sure that you never see the inside of this building or any of the family properties. I'll manage the company's money and I'll insist that Mom reduces how much of it you receive each year. Or, we can buy you out of this family and you can spend your inheritance now, eventually running out of money by the time you're fifty years old."

Wyatt wasn't smiling any longer. The smirk on his face was gone, and his skin was pale. Clayton looked like he was going to be sick.

"You wouldn't dare," Wyatt responded.

"Try me," Trevor said. "It's your choice, Wyatt. I'm trying to get you exactly what you want…money. The only difference is that you'll have to earn it like the rest of us. So, what's it going to be?"

Wyatt didn't answer.

Trevor got up from the sofa and walked to the door. "I'll see you Thursday morning at nine in the morning ready to meet with the architect. If you're not there, I'll know what you've decided to do."

He walked out of the office and to the receptionist's desk.

"Janet, I want you to call a locksmith and tell them we need someone here after hours to change the lock on Dad's office door."

Janet seemed to understand Trevor's frustration and anger, which, in his opinion, was a good thing. The sooner the rest of the employees grasped the seriousness of his dislike for Wyatt the better.

If Wyatt was going to cause trouble, it was best everyone recognize it from the start. Transparency was the best way he knew to build a case against his brother, and Trevor needed to be ready to remove Wyatt from the building at a moment's notice.

At Jeff's request, Michael and Christopher met him at The Lodge Fork Brewery Company to talk about Lauren. Frustrated that his wife dismissed most of his concerns about her health, he thought her brothers might have some advice about how best to deal with the stress and his feelings of helplessness.

"I really appreciate you guys meeting me like this. I'm at my wit's end."

"It's understandable. Chris and I had to seek professional help to get through our trauma. Maybe that's what Lauren needs as well," Michael offered.

"Yeah, but the two of you were visibly suffering, I mean everyone could see it. With Lauren, she's acting like nothing ever happened. This morning she pulled off all the bandages and put makeup on the small scar on her face. It's like she's trying to erase any memory of the fire. Even when we talk about the investigation, she changes the subject."

"She's in denial so that behavior makes perfect sense," Chris said.

"Yeah, I get it. What I don't know is what to do about it. Your mother's been calling me every day to see how she's doing and I feel bad that I keep saying everything is just fine."

"Why are you doing that?" Michael asked.

"Because I know Maggie. If I tell her the truth she'll get on a plane faster than the blink of an eye."

Christopher shrugged. "Maybe Mom can help. She helped me and Michael."

"I don't know. I do know that a bunch of her friends from up here are going down to Captiva to have a bachelorette party, and then there's talk of her and Paolo going to Italy for Ciara's wedding. Even if I did tell Maggie the truth, I'd hate to mess all that up."

Michael nodded. "Well, you're right about that. Mom would cancel all of it and fly up here. However, I do think that we better tell Beth and Sarah. They'd kill us if we didn't update them on Lauren's situation. They must be calling you all the time."

"Beth has called three times and Sarah twice. They both have lots on their plate, but you're right. It's their sister after all. Maybe they might have some ideas as well."

"I know that Beth helped me a lot after my leg was amputated. When I went to stay with Mom in Captiva, Beth flew down and stayed with me. She and I had some of the best conversations of our lives."

Michael nodded. "She talked to me on the phone from California after I got shot. Beth's got a talent for seeing things that others can't. I don't know what I would have done without our little sister's advice. It's true, she might be able to help Lauren more than any of us."

"Michael's got a good point, however, I think you need to get Lauren to talk to a professional. If she's in denial it will be that much harder for any of us to reach her. She needs someone who knows how to get through to her," Christopher said.

"I agree but getting her to talk to someone might be harder than we think," Jeff said. "She's spending every moment getting ready to reopen her agency in a new location."

"Where is her new place?" Michael asked.

"Over on Sutton Rd. It's on the first floor of a medical building. There are a few non-medical businesses in the building and she was lucky to get space on the first floor. That will help promote the agency."

"Hey, *my* therapist is in that building," Michael said. "Maybe I could talk to her about Lauren."

"Yeah, that would work except that there still isn't anything she can do if Lauren won't talk to her," Jeff pointed out.

"What if they talk to each other as tenants in the building first? Dr. Wells could welcome Lauren to the building. They could talk and once Lauren feels comfortable with her she might decide on her own to talk about the fire," Michael said.

"That could work," Christopher said.

Jeff nodded. "Well, it's the only way I can see her talking to a professional. The doctor won't be able to force Lauren to do anything she doesn't want to do. It would have to feel natural."

Michael nodded. "I agree. I think it could work. I'm seeing Dr. Wells tomorrow. I'll run it by her and see what she thinks of the idea. Between her and Beth, and maybe even Sarah, we might get Lauren the best help she could ever ask for...a professional, and, as always, her family."

"I really appreciate it, Michael. Let me know soon, will you? I'm really worried about her and the baby."

"Will do. In the meantime, if you need anything please call either of us," Michael said. "That's the beauty of living so close to one another, and something I know that Mom depends on now that she's so far away and can't be here when a crisis arises."

Jeff nodded. "Do me a favor, will you guys? Please don't tell Grandma Sarah about this. The last thing we need is for her to get into the mix. The whole situation is complicated and I know that sometimes Grandma thinks there's a simple solution to everything."

Christopher laughed. "That's Grandma for you. Most of her advice falls under the 'put your big girl pants on, or when I was a young girl'...fill in the blank."

"Exactly," Jeff said. "This is one of those times when tough love won't cut it. Besides, Maggie would kill us if we told Grandma and not her."

"Not only that but Grandma is closing on her house in two weeks. If she thought things were really bad here, she might cancel that and not move to Florida," Michael added.

"That's one thing that Grandma and your mother have in common. Both of them want to solve their children's problems by hovering and controlling everything," Jeff said.

Michael and Christopher laughed at that. "Well, Mom had to learn it somewhere."

CHAPTER 13

"Are you sure you're all right?" Millie asked Matteo as she helped him to the chair. "You have to be careful on these stairs."

His breathing labored and perspiration showing on his ashen face, Matteo grabbed the armrest and tried to steady himself.

"I'm fine now, thank you, Millie. I think I'll rest here for a few minutes."

Millie took his backpack and put it on the floor next to him. "I think you need to rest for longer than a few minutes," she said.

He shook his head. "No, I have an appointment later. If I rest for a bit, I'll be fine to go. Thank you for your concern."

Millie wasn't convinced that Matteo was fine at all. This wasn't the first time that he was unsteady on his feet. If not for the cane, she didn't think he'd be able to walk at all.

"How about I go with you to your appointment?" she asked.

He shook his head. "No, thank you. Honestly, you're making too big a fuss about this. It was just a small slip. I can manage on my own."

There was little Millie could do to prevent him from going to his appointment, but she felt uncomfortable leaving him alone.

"How about I sit with you for a bit? What time is your appointment?"

He hesitated but answered her, "Eleven o'clock."

"How far away is it? Do you need someone to drive you?"

Matteo appeared to lose patience with her.

"Millie, I don't want to be rude and I don't mind if we sit here a spell, however, I'd like you to leave me to my business...please."

She wasn't offended, but she could tell that getting Matteo to trust her would be difficult if not impossible.

"Can I get you something to drink?" she asked.

"A glass of water would be nice, thank you."

"Do you want ice in it?"

"No. Just water."

She quickly went into the kitchen and returned with a tall glass of water.

He drank the water in several long gulps and handed the empty glass to Millie. "Thank you very much. I think I'm much better now."

Matteo picked up his backpack, rose from the chair and leaned on his cane. He looked up at the sky. "It looks to be a beautiful day. I must be going now. Thank you, Millie. I do appreciate your concern, but I'll be just fine. You have a nice day and I'll see you when I get back."

He slowly walked down the stairs, being careful not to trip, and then continued down the driveway and out onto the street.

Millie watched him turn left and walk toward Andy Rosse Lane and the taxi that would no doubt be waiting for him.

Shaking her head, she went back inside and then sat on a kitchen island stool.

Looking at Riley, Millie said, "I wish I knew what that man is doing. He should be resting in bed."

"I know. He doesn't look well at all. He asked Iris to make him a sandwich and asked if we had an apple or piece of fruit he could have. We pretty much stuffed his backpack as if he was going on a picnic," Riley said.

"A picnic? There is no way that man should be going on a picnic. How in the world would he even get up off the ground? And I don't believe him when he says that he has an appointment at eleven. I don't think he's meeting anyone at all."

"What do you think he's doing when he leaves here?" Maggie asked as she came into the kitchen.

Millie shook her head. "I have no idea. I wanted to follow him when he first got here, but then I figured that if he caught me, he might give the inn a negative review. I didn't want to risk it."

Maggie shrugged. "Well, it's really none of our business. We have to leave the man alone to do whatever he wants."

"Maggie, he almost fell on the back porch stairs. I had to help him and stayed with him until he got his strength back."

Worried, Maggie put her hand to her chest. "Oh my, is he all right? What happened?"

"He says it was just a slip and that he's fine, but he looks sick. His face was sweaty and his body shook when I helped him to a chair. He would only take a glass of water and a little rest before heading out. I tried to get him to let me take him to his appointment but he said no. He thanked me and said he didn't want to be rude but basically wanted to be left alone."

Maggie nodded. "Well then, that is exactly what we're going to do. In the meantime, we all have work to get to, so I suggest we get to it. Millie, I've got a number of invoices I need you to add into the computer. I've left them on my desk. If you could update the books that would be great. I'm off to the carriage house to call Lauren. I've waited long enough to hear from my daughter. It's time she hears from her mother whether she wants to or not."

"Mom! It's so great to hear from you. I was going to call you but I've been so busy. I know you've heard about the fire."

"Yes, honey, I did. I thought you'd call me by now," Maggie said.

"Oh, you can't imagine how busy I've been. Nell, Brian and I finally found a great location for the new office, so we've been busy getting that up and running. I've had to buy all new furniture and computers which is a hassle, but it has to be done."

"Lauren, how are you feeling? I've been very worried about you and the baby."

"We're fine, Mom. I just had my five-month appointment with my obstetrician. Everything is looking good."

Maggie remembered Sarah's conversation with Beth and looked for anything in Lauren's voice that might confirm everyone's worry.

"What about Nell and Brian? How are they doing?"

"Great. Thankfully they weren't hurt. You know, Mom, I think the whole thing was a blessing in disguise."

"What do you mean?"

"Well, I didn't really like our landlord. He was difficult to deal with and I had to call him all the time to fix the leak in the bathroom. I'm glad we're in this new medical building. Everything is new and modern."

Lauren's last comment was the sign Maggie was looking for. To say that the fire was a blessing in disguise when two young people lost their lives was heartless at best and contrary to Lauren's usual empathetic and compassionate nature.

Maggie had no choice but to admonish her daughter.

"Tell that to the Murphys. I understand that Shannon was their only child. I think it's a cruel thing for you to say the fire was a blessing when two innocent people with their whole lives ahead of them perished. Nothing about that fire was a blessing, not even for you, Lauren, and I'm surprised to hear you saying so."

Lauren's silence was proof to Maggie that she'd hit a nerve. After what seemed like a few minutes, Maggie felt there was nothing more she could say.

"I have to go. Give my love to Jeff and the girls."

"Mom! Wait!" Lauren yelled into the phone. "I'm sorry, I didn't mean to be so glib. I feel terrible about what's happened. It's just that I feel a strong urge to move forward and I'm afraid… I just can't…"

Lauren seemed unable to finish her thought. Maggie sensed her daughter's pain but also the need to hang on to whatever normalcy she could.

"Lauren, I know this is hard. You've been through something terrifying and I can't imagine what that feels like. I just want you not to push your feelings away so you don't have to look at it. I've been there and I know what it's like to paint a pretty picture of a life that isn't real. You can't change what happened, but you can be a better person for it."

She couldn't remember the last time she'd ever spoken to one of her children this way and she was certain that it hurt her just as much as it did Lauren, but it had to be said.

"I've got to go, Mom. Can we talk later?"

"Of course. If I don't hear from you in a couple of days, I'll call you again."

Maggie knew that Lauren had listened to everything she said, but she could also feel the urgency to get off the phone and end this discussion.

Her heart broke at the thought that Lauren was deeply in denial from the pain and trauma of the fire. She worried that if her daughter didn't get help, and soon, there was no telling what she'd do to avoid grieving. Lauren's stoic behavior would eventually fall away, it was only a matter of when and how that would happen.

As a mother she wanted to do more but her hands were tied. She'd make phone calls to her other children, and offer recommendations, but only Lauren could ask for help. Without that, her pain and denial would deepen, and no one would be able to reach her.

That thought more than any other terrified Maggie. She put her hand to her heart and closed her eyes remembering Lauren as a baby. She rocked back and forth as if to hold her child. Then, without warning, the tears fell and Maggie sunk into the sofa and wept.

Riley watched the comings and goings around her as she carefully and slowly opened the oven. She'd made four small soufflés for the first time in months and wanted to test her recipe before Maggie's party.

She remembered that her mother used to tell her that loud noises could make a soufflé drop, but so far, Riley had never experienced that phenomenon. Besides, she couldn't very well tell everyone to stop opening and shutting doors. Mr. Benedetti clearly needed help and Riley hoped soon they'd get to the bottom of whatever was making him ill.

The kitchen island was covered with bowls, eggs, flour, both regular and powdered sugar, and butter. The soufflés were plain without additional flavorings like raspberries or chocolate, but she planned to experiment more if these four were a success.

"Those look amazing," Millie said.

"Thanks. I think they came out great," Riley said as she sprinkled powdered sugar on top of each soufflé.

"Have you ever considered opening your own bakery? I mean you are seriously talented."

Riley laughed. "I appreciate the compliment, Millie, but I'm pretty sure Maggie wouldn't like that one bit."

Millie dismissed the remark with a wave of her hand. "Don't be silly. Maggie would want the very best for you. If owning your own bakery was your dream I bet she'd be behind you one hundred percent."

It was a knee-jerk reaction, but Riley had always struggled with trusting Millie's motivations. The suspicion came from months ago when Millie first came into the Key Lime Garden Inn and pretended to be someone other than who she was.

Since Millie had always believed her father to be Robert Lane, the owner of the Key Lime Garden Inn back in the 1960s, she set about threatening Maggie and Paolo by saying she was truly the inn's owner due to inheritance.

Fortunately for the Morettis, Robert never owned the property, and Millie turned out not to be his daughter. There were hard feelings all around, but the Morettis forgave Millie and welcomed her into their home and business. Millie had become part of the inn's family, but Riley still felt uneasy talking to her.

"Are you trying to get rid of me, Millie?" Riley asked.

"Oh, my goodness, no. Absolutely not. I'd hate to see you go. I'm just saying that your cooking is really spectacular, especially your desserts."

Riley smiled. "Well, thank you. I'm glad you like my food, but I'll be staying here at the inn for the time being. I like working here. What about you? How are things going for you now that you've been back a few months?"

"Honestly, I'm happier than I've been in a very long time. I have the Morettis to thank for that. I'd love to buy a condo on the island, but it's really hard. Everything is so expensive and very much out of my price range. Do you live on Captiva?"

"No, I live in Sanibel, but my sister Grace and I grew up there. I know what you mean about real estate prices. You can find some good rentals, but to buy, it will cost you."

A few minutes of silence passed between them before Millie spoke. "You don't like me much do you Riley?"

Stunned that she'd been so transparent, Riley was taken aback. "Why do you say that?"

Millie shrugged. "You seem to keep your distance from me. I know I put the Morettis through a lot but we've moved on. I'm grateful for their forgiveness and trust. I hope to earn yours as well."

"I'm sorry, Millie. I didn't realize that you felt this way. I guess I do still feel conflicted about you, but then again, I'm not easily trusting of people. It takes time before I let my guard down."

Millie nodded. "Well, time we've got. Perhaps that's all we need."

Riley smiled, opened a drawer and handed Millie a spoon. She pushed one of the soufflés in front of Millie and grabbed a spoon for herself.

"Here you go. Let's start by sharing this soufflé. I need another person's opinion before I serve these to Maggie's guests next week."

Millie smiled and clinked her spoon against Riley's.

It was a small gesture, but an important one. Sharing her beloved creation was the best way Riley knew to take the first step toward her renewed friendship with Millie. Where they went from here was anyone's guess, but she was pleased to feel a glimmer of forgiveness right around the corner.

CHAPTER 14

Maggie watched Chelsea clean her paint brushes and finally asked the question she'd been dying to for the last several weeks. "You know, I've been very quiet about not mentioning Carlo, but since you're not talking I'm going to have to ask. Are the two of you still dating?"

Chelsea made a face that Maggie couldn't decipher. "What does that face mean?"

"It means I was happier before, when you were quiet and not so inquisitive," Chelsea answered.

"Come on. I tell you everything. What's going on between the two of you?"

"Nothing is going on, that's the problem. I didn't really think of him as my boyfriend. He was more of someone to go out with when I didn't have anything else going on. But, after a while, and, I'm ashamed to say this, I started to like him more and more."

"So, what's the problem?"

"He broke up with me, said he was seeing someone else and it was turning serious. I'm not heartbroken about it, just disappointed because I was getting used to him being around."

"A younger woman?" Maggie asked.

"Really, Maggie? Did you have to go there?"

"I'm sorry, Chelsea. It happens to women our age all the time."

"Well, it didn't happen to me. He didn't leave me for a younger woman. He left me for an older one, one with a lot more money."

Maggie tried not to laugh, but from the moment Maggie met Carlo she knew his dating Chelsea would be short-lived. Not because Chelsea was a lot older than him, but because he appeared to be a player…someone who bounced around from woman to woman with no intention of settling down.

"Did I mention that he's getting married? That's what happens when you don't want to lose all that money. You've got to move fast before she comes to her senses and changes her mind," she said.

"Oh, you can't believe she's not going to have a prenup? I mean with someone like Carlo she better protect her assets."

Maggie looked at her friend and smiled. "You don't seem too upset about it though."

Pensive, Chelsea answered her, "I guess I'm not. I think I liked that his name was almost like Carl's."

Maggie laughed. "Don't think I didn't think of that. Carlo was really handsome, but I wondered if you went out with him because of his name. I know that sounds silly, but…"

Chelsea shrugged. "I've done sillier things."

"Haven't we all?" Maggie said. "I've been meaning to ask you something. Did you notice anything unusual about Diana during our video get-together the other day?"

"You mean about her looking sad? I wondered about that myself so I called her," Chelsea said.

"When were you going to tell me that? I thought we were best friends," Maggie teased.

"I was getting around to telling you. We've all been a little busy lately if you remember."

"Well? What did she say?"

"She said that she's been miserable ever since she retired. She keeps trying to fill her days with things but nothing feels exciting anymore."

"That's awful. I wish there was something we could suggest. Any ideas?"

"I haven't a clue. I mean her marriage is fine, although she said that her husband doesn't ever want to do anything except work on his antique cars. They went to Greece a couple of months ago, and he kept complaining that the sun was too strong. He wore a hat everywhere, which any other time wouldn't have been such a big deal, but apparently now, everything he does annoys her."

"Well, Charlie never was very exciting."

"True enough. Anyway, I asked her if maybe she should go back to work. She loved what she was doing and had built up such a brand. Everyone loved her bakery and even thought she should write a cookbook. I told her I thought that was a great idea."

"What did she say?"

"If you can believe it, she has already put one together. She showed it to me on Zoom. It's a good-sized book. There were tons of yellow sticky notes in it because she said it needs editing, but otherwise it's ready to go. I encouraged her to finish the book and consider going back to work, but she just put the book down and shrugged her shoulders as if she'd get to it one day."

"A cookbook! What a great idea. I love that I know someone who's published a cookbook...well, almost published. I'm going to text her and ask her to bring what she's put together to Captiva. Maybe if we all look at it and encourage her, she'll finish the book sooner rather than later," Maggie said.

"I have an even better idea," Chelsea added. "How about she adds a few recipes from all of us? We're fairly good cooks, and I know we've each got several recipes that we've created ourselves that she could add."

Maggie clapped her hands together. "Oh, Chelsea, do you

think she'll do it? I love that idea. Maybe I can add my scones with the vegan clotted cream."

Chelsea laughed. "Are you kidding? Of course, you absolutely must include your scones. People talk about how fantastic they are all the time. If you want my opinion, they're the best I've ever had."

Whatever the plan, Maggie loved the idea of helping Diana get out of her funk and was certain that the party on Captiva was the magic pill they all needed to reconnect once again.

Sarah had already scheduled several activities but it was Maggie who couldn't wait to tell everyone about her plan to bring her friends together in a new and exciting way.

Trevor's sisters Jacqui and Carolyn sat on the sofa in the den and kept Devon company for all of ten minutes before they both looked awkward and bored.

"Why don't you read something to your father? He loves reading and we've got plenty of books on these bookshelves," Eliza said.

"Mother, I've got to get back to the kids. I just wanted to stop in and see how Dad is getting along. I think he's better, don't you?"

Jacqui rolled her eyes since it was perfectly obvious to anyone who cared to look that their father wasn't better at all. In fact, except for Trevor, Jacqui seemed the most concerned about her father's situation out of all of his children.

"You'd better get going then," Jacqui said, hoping to have her father all to herself.

The sour look on Carolyn's face wasn't new. Her sister always looked slightly perturbed.

Carolyn picked up her handbag, kissed Devon on the forehead and then looked at Jacqui.

"What are your plans? When do you have to get back to New York?"

"I don't. If you remember, I've just graduated. I've got to look for a job soon, but there's no rush. I'd prefer to stay here until Dad improves."

Jacqui could tell that Carolyn didn't care one bit what her plans were. Instead, her sister, much like her brothers Wyatt and Clayton, was a spoiled, selfish and self-centered person who was constantly judging her status in whatever room she occupied.

Carolyn looked at Devon once more. "I hate to say this, Jacqui, but you might want to rethink that."

The implication was cruel. Just because their father couldn't talk didn't mean he couldn't hear or understand. The fact that Carolyn expected Devon to die and said so in front of him was another of her insensitive and hurtful behaviors.

"I don't think it's productive to speculate on Dad's condition like that. I think he's been showing improvement."

Carolyn scoffed and muttered something under her breath as she headed towards the door.

Jacqui shook her head at her sister's lack of empathy, and then looked at her father. She moved closer to him and held his hand. She didn't expect an answer, but needed to ask him a question, nonetheless.

"What is it about this family that makes everyone incapable of true affection and kindness?"

She felt movement in her hands and when she looked down could tell that he was trying to communicate with her. She looked in his eyes and was sure that the left corner of his lips moved upward as if to smile.

Jacqui smiled at her father. "You can understand me, can't you?"

She leaned closer and kissed his cheek. "You're going to get better, Dad. You'll show them."

She got up and pulled out a book from the bookcase. Determined to help her father recover, she decided to read to him. She figured that she had to do something...anything rather than sit and wait for her father to die. No matter how much time they had, she'd make the most of it so that when his time came, she'd have no regrets.

After two hours with her father, Jacqui decided to drive to Captiva to see her boyfriend, Joshua Powell. The drive brought back happy memories of the summer Jacqui lived with Chelsea Marsden and learned to perfect painting watercolor landscapes.

Along the way she formed a friendship and romance with Crawford Powell's son. They didn't see each other often since Jacqui had to finish graduate school in New York City, but their friendship deepened and now that she'd graduated she had to think about her future. Whether to stay in New York, or to move back home to Florida, Jacqui needed the kind of clarity that only Joshua could give her.

"Hey, handsome," she called out as she pulled her car in front of Powell Water Sports."

Joshua ran to her car and stuck his head inside to give her a kiss. "How'd it go? How's your father doing?"

"I think he's getting better. His hand moved and I swear he smiled at me," she said getting out of her car.

"That's great news. So, any chance you might go to Italy with me at the end of the month?"

"What? Is this a joke?"

Joshua shook his head. "No joke. My dad and Ciara have decided to get married in Italy instead of Captiva. We're all going. I thought maybe you'd like to be my date."

"Oh, right. I've heard about this. My sister-in-law Sarah is the Maid of Honor. To be honest, I'm not sure what's going on. Trevor said that Sarah might not go even though he told her to.

Trevor definitely can't, and now with my father improving, I don't feel like I can be that far away. My sister Carolyn visited for about thirty minutes, Clayton and Wyatt are so self-absorbed it's hard to imagine they'll devote much time with Dad. Trevor is so busy trying to keep everything up and running, I feel like I'm Dad's best chance to let him know how much we want him to get better."

"Doesn't he get therapy of some kind?" Joshua asked.

"I'll say he does. Two different nurses attend to him and a couple of therapists a week come. I think one deals with his cognitive rehab and the other, physical stuff. I don't know much about it but I do know that they're trying to get him to talk."

"Does he understand you when you talk to him?"

Jacqui nodded. "I think he definitely does."

"Then why not explain to him about the wedding. Tell him that you'll only be gone a few days...less than a week. Will you think about it?"

Jacqui adored the idea of traveling to Italy with Joshua. The artwork alone would be worth the trip, but to spend quality time with her boyfriend in a romantic city was a dream she'd love to experience. The trip would also give them time to talk about the future of their relationship.

"I will. Let me see if I can talk Sarah into going too. I know she's got the kids but she's kept the nanny to help out here and there. Maybe if Ciara, Trevor and I put pressure on her to go, she'll cave."

Joshua smiled. "I like the way you think."

CHAPTER 15

Grandma Sarah stayed out of Lauren's way but checked in several times since the fire. Lauren's struggles were evident to everyone and no one seemed willing to talk about it with Grandma Sarah.

She couldn't tell who decided it was best to keep her out of the loop, but if she had to guess, she suspected her grandchildren.

She had Christopher, Becca, Michael, Brea and their children over for dinner and Beth and Gabriel joined them for dessert since Beth had to work late. Lauren and Jeff couldn't make it because Olivia had a dance recital.

Several times during the evening Grandma Sarah noticed everyone stopped talking the minute she walked into the room. After the third time she'd had enough.

"Okay, that's it. Who is going to explain what's going on?"

Beth and Christopher looked at each other, and Michael cleared his throat, a sign that Grandma Sarah took as confirmation of her suspicions.

Beth spoke first. "We believe that Lauren isn't dealing well with what happened the day of the fire."

"What does that mean?"

"It means that she's almost going out of her way to be upbeat, cheerful and won't talk about the fire. Jeff says she hasn't cried once, and hardly took any time to rest and heal before going right back to work," Christopher said. "He's worried."

"So are we," Becca added.

Grandma Sarah took a minute to understand the situation. She pulled a chair out from the table and sat before responding.

"You all think you're psychiatrists now? What makes you think she's not dealing with things? Are you privy to her private moments? None of us have any idea what it must have been like to almost die in that fire, but I can imagine it was terrifying. Not to mention she's carrying a life inside her. However, none of this has anything to do with why you all didn't come to me about this sooner. Why so secretive?"

"Grandma, you're closing on your house and new condo in Florida next week. We were worried that you might not go, that you might stay in Massachusetts to help Lauren. We thought it best not to say anything," Michael answered.

"Well you thought wrong. Here's some food for thought. Everyone grieves in their own way and in their own time. I understand how close this family is and how we're in each other's business all the time…maybe even too much by some people's standards. You know me, I don't care what people think, but I do care that what this family has risks being lost if we don't talk to one another. I'm still going to Florida because I can't help anyone if I don't take care of myself, but that doesn't mean I'm ignoring your sister's needs."

"Sorry, Grandma," Beth said. "You're right, we should have told you what's been going on. Just remember that we were also trying to protect you as well."

Grandma Sarah reached across the table and took Beth's hand. Looking around the table, she could feel her grandchildren's love and protection.

"I love you all, but don't forget, I'm pretty good at taking care of myself. Some say I'm...what's that word?"

"Formidable?" Christopher answered.

"Yeah, that's it...formidable. That's me in a nutshell. Now, let's eat."

Grandma Sarah loved having her family over for dinner but was sad that this one would be their last for a while. She soon would be on a plane to Captiva and her daughter Maggie, and she couldn't wait.

However, she had one more thing to do before leaving, and it would involve an afternoon with her granddaughter Lauren.

Grandma Sarah had a plan. It didn't take much investigation to know that Maggie must be beside herself over Lauren's situation. To be so far away when one of her children was struggling was Maggie's worst nightmare, and Grandma Sarah knew it.

It wasn't elaborate or difficult to implement, but it meant that she'd have to pretend that she was afraid of moving to Florida without family by her side. Since the behavior went against everything she'd told Beth, Christopher and Michael, she'd have to let them in on her little scheme.

The first thing she needed was to talk to Maggie about Lauren. She didn't waste any time so as soon as her grandchildren left she called Maggie.

"Hey, Mom, is everything all right?" Maggie asked.

"No, everything is not all right. Are you aware of what Lauren is going through?"

She could hear Maggie sigh. "Yes, I have some idea and it's driving me crazy. What can I do? I can't fly up there right now because my lunch-bunch friends are all coming down for a bachelorette party that I'm in charge of and I feel guilty as..."

"Well, you should feel guilty. This is your daughter we're

talking about. You should have let someone else handle the party. What does Sarah say about all this?"

"Both Sarah and I feel terrible about it, but what can we do? I mean I've talked to Michael and Jeff and they both seem to think that Lauren is in good hands. I can't storm up there and take control of the situation. If Lauren isn't facing the situation, she'd be furious with me for sticking my nose where it doesn't belong."

"Don't be ridiculous. That's what mothers do. We stick our noses in where they don't belong all the time. I have experience in this department. Kids always act like they don't want their parents to interfere, but it's not really true."

When Maggie didn't respond to her comment, Grandma Sarah got to the point.

"Well, anyway, I'm just saying that something ought to be done about this."

"I agree," Maggie said. "I'll call Jeff tomorrow and see what he says. I'll have a couple of weeks between the party and going to Italy. I can probably come up sometime then."

Frustrated with her daughter, Grandma Sarah couldn't believe her ears. Lauren needed her mother and instead of taking care of business, Maggie was throwing parties and flying off to Italy.

"Italy? Why are you going to Italy?"

"Ciara is getting married and Paolo will give her away."

"Oh, I see. Well, of course you have to do that. He's her brother after all. I guess there's nothing to be done about that."

"On another note, are you all set with flying down here at the end of next week?"

"I'm fine. Don't worry about me. Will your friends still be there when I arrive?"

"No, they're leaving the day before you get in. It's too bad you won't get to see them all," Maggie said.

"Maggie dear, they all live in Massachusetts. If they wanted to see me they'd come around. I don't need to fly to Captiva to see them."

She could hear Maggie's exasperation and thought it best to end the call.

"Maggie, I've got a million things to do before I get to Florida. I'll talk to you before I leave."

When she ended the call, Grandma Sarah thought about the timeline for the next week. There was much to do if she was going to help Lauren and very little time.

The equation was simple. Lauren needed her mother and Maggie needed her daughter, so if it took a little white lie to get the two of them together, so be it.

Wyatt did more than show up for work that Thursday. For several days after their first meeting, Trevor noticed that his brother attended office meetings and even went to check in on the new development project several times.

Trevor was cautiously optimistic as Wyatt never did anything without getting something in return. As difficult as Wyatt could be, Trevor recognized something in his brother that bonded them. Both had issues with their father growing up, and both chose a different path initially just to get away from him.

Trevor found his way back to the family business and eventually made peace with his father. He'd come to respect all that Devon had accomplished in his life. Now that Wyatt had returned, albeit temporarily, Trevor hoped the same would happen for his brother.

Whether Wyatt would continue to do the right thing was anyone's guess, but, for now at least, there was cooperation amongst the brothers.

"Knock, knock," Jacqui said, standing in Trevor's office doorway.

He looked up from his paperwork and smiled. He was especially fond of his sister and although she had her own demons to deal with growing up, she'd worked hard to find her place in the world and stopped her partying ways.

"Hey, sis. Come in. This is a first. When was the last time you were in this building?"

"Hmmm, hard to say. It could have been the time I stopped in to ask Dad for money, or maybe it was the time I had a little too much to drink and wanted Dad to finally disown me so he'd leave me alone. I might have vomited in his office if I remember correctly. I don't think I've been in this office since."

Trevor laughed. "Ah, your teenage years. I bet they were filled with all kinds of adventures just to drive our parents crazy."

Jacqui nodded. "I guess I was a handful. I don't know why he never totally gave up on me."

Trevor thought Jacqui seemed sad. "What's got you down? I can tell something is wrong."

She smiled. "You always could tell when something was bothering me. It's nothing so shocking as the old days, I'm just really worried about Dad. When I was at the house with him the other day, he moved his hand and tried to smile at me."

"I heard. That's progress, honey. I think he'll continue to improve over time. The doctor said that when he finally stops making progress, then that's what he'll live with. He's not done fighting, Jacqui."

"I hope not. Listen, there's another reason I decided to come see you in the office instead of your house. I really want you to go to Italy with Sarah. Not just because she's Ciara's Maid of Honor, but because I think you can trust Wyatt and Clayton to handle things for a few days. Besides, it's possible that I might go too."

"You're going to Italy? Did Ciara invite you?"

"No, the groom's son, Joshua did."

Trevor nodded. "Oh, right. I forgot that the two of you were seeing each other. I think that's fantastic that you're going. As far as me leaving Wyatt and Clayton to run things…I'm not so sure."

"Oh for heaven's sake, Trevor. What in the world do you think Wyatt is going to do? He doesn't get a dime if the place goes under. He's got a vested interest in seeing this business succeed."

"True enough, but what about Dad? Do you think Wyatt will start venting to him? Dad's progress involves keeping his stress level down. I don't trust that Wyatt won't take this opportunity to bring his complaints to Dad now that he can't really respond."

"That's a terrible thing to say," Jacqui insisted. "What you're implying is that Wyatt could actually kill Dad doing that. If you really feel that way, then why in the world would you risk it by asking him to come back? You had to take a leap of faith in Wyatt to do that. Am I right?"

Trevor felt ashamed that he even suggested his brother would do their father harm. He wasn't even sure where that thought came from. Things were progressing nicely between Wyatt and the rest of the family. How could he even suggest such a thing?

He shook his head. "I don't know why I said that. I didn't mean that Wyatt could be so cruel. I mean he's been wild and immature but that doesn't mean he's evil. It's just that I know Wyatt isn't finished with Dad, nor should he be if there's going to be healing between them. It's just that Dad is in no condition to hear negative accusations right now. Maybe once he's back to normal, they can talk about such things, but not now."

"I agree," she said. "Will you seriously think about Italy? Sarah would be so happy."

Trevor smiled. Since she was a child Jacqui was always able to get Trevor to do whatever she asked. "I'll think about it."

She clapped her hands. "Perfect. I've got to run. Don't take too long to think about this. The wedding will be here before you know it."

CHAPTER 16

Riley couldn't help watching Mr. Benedetti from the kitchen window. He'd taken a slow walk around the building and when he came upon the rose bushes near the fence, he looked up at her and waved.

After his second time around, he walked up onto the back porch to sit. Seeming winded, Riley was concerned about him.

"Mr. Benedetti are you all right? Can I get you something?" she asked.

He wiped his forehead with a small face cloth he'd kept in his pocket.

"No, thank you, Riley. I just need to sit for a spell."

She nodded and was going to go back into the kitchen but decided instead to spend some time with him.

"Do you mind if I join you?" she asked.

"Not at all. Please."

He moved over to give her room to sit on the porch swing with him. The swing was large enough for two people but no more than that.

Riley looked up at the sky. "It certainly is one of the prettiest days we've had lately. You've come to Captiva at a good time. I know it's hot and summer can be brutal here, but right before it gets so hot that you want to stay inside with air conditioning the days can be beautiful. I guess that's true in a lot of places. That must be why there are so many June brides."

He smiled and nodded. "I think you're right. Are you married, Riley?"

She laughed to herself. Even a stranger like Mr. Benedetti went right to the question of the day. She smiled at him and then teased him a little. "Have you been talking to my mother?"

He didn't get the joke and answered her, "No, should I have?"

"I'm just saying that question is a sore spot between me and my mother. She wants me to get married and start having babies right away. I think the problem is hers more than it is mine."

"Well, perhaps she just wants grandchildren."

"That's it exactly. She's even said so right to my face."

"What did you tell her?" he asked.

"I told her that I'm not a baby-making machine, and that I'll get married in time but not before I fall in love."

He nodded. "That seems to be a normal response. You must have love if you're going to spend the rest of your life with someone. Imagine feeling like you couldn't live without the other person. I think the feeling should be as strong as that."

"I see that you're wearing a wedding ring, Mr. Benedetti…"

"Please call me Matteo, and yes, I'm a married man."

"But you're here alone. Where is your wife?"

"In the Fort Myers Memorial Cemetery. She passed away eighteen months ago."

"Oh, I'm so sorry. I didn't mean…"

He patted her hand. "I know, dear. I haven't spoken about Louise to anyone really. It's been a difficult and long eighteen months."

"I bet. There's nothing to compare to losing someone you love. It's a heartbreak for sure. It must be very difficult to be here on Captiva without her by your side."

Riley waited for his response, but he never answered her. It was almost as if he didn't hear anything she said. She didn't want to press and mention his wife again.

"How long have you been working here at the inn, Riley?"

"Four years now," she answered.

"Do you love your job?" he asked.

It seemed a strange question to ask. No one had ever asked her this before and she never thought much about whether she loved her job or not. She knew that she was good at it and wanted to keep creating delicious meals for people, but beyond that she couldn't express her feelings about working at the Key Lime Garden Inn.

"I hadn't thought about it before, but I do like the Morettis and I like how everyone who works here is family. It's a community of people who want to represent the very best of Captiva. I think that's important."

He nodded. "It is very important. I know that you've made my time here very special."

Her smile grew. "Well thank you, Matteo. That's very kind of you to say."

"It's as if every member of the staff weaves their specific talents and time into the fabric of what makes this inn special. You all need to own that. It's important. You don't just work for the Morettis, you help them create a place of solitude and respite, at least that's what you've done for me. You should feel proud."

Riley wanted to cry. It was easy to feel comfortable in her position, but Matteo's words helped her see the importance of her role at the Key Lime Garden Inn.

She put her arms around Matteo and hugged him. "Thank you, Matteo. You've made my day, maybe even my year. I've got to get back to the kitchen. If I'm going to make a real difference I'd better get to it. I'm glad we could spend some time together. You have a good day and let me know if you need or want anything. You know where to find me."

"The kitchen, right?" he said, trying to make a joke.

She laughed. "Exactly."

Lauren's first panic attack came in the middle of the night. She woke from a terrible nightmare, pulled the blanket up to her chin, and took several deep breaths.

"You're safe," Jeff whispered as he held her in his arms. "Everything is fine. The kids are good, the baby is healthy.

"I can't breathe," she choked.

"Yes, you can. Put your hand on your chest and we'll breathe together," Jeff said.

She did as he instructed and, following his whispers, began to take slow, deliberate breaths. She could feel her heart racing but after a few minutes it regained its normal pace.

Jeff wiped Lauren's forehead with his hand and pulled her head onto his shoulder. She felt safe in his arms but wondered when the next attack would come. It was bad enough to experience such terror in her sleep, but another to be awake and anticipating doom around the corner.

"I can't live like this," she said.

Her words created a panic in his own body, but he tried to stay calm and looked for the positive. He placed his hand on her belly.

"I beg to differ. This little guy in here might have a thing or two to say about that."

"What kind of a mother am I?"

Confused, Jeff couldn't understand what Lauren was asking him.

"What a question. If you ask Olivia and Lily, I'm pretty sure they'll tell you that you're the best mother in the world. What makes you think otherwise?"

All she could do was shake her head and close her eyes. She

never answered him and Jeff continued to reassure her that she was a wonderful mother.

"Come on, lay back on the pillow and keep your hand on your chest. You'll fall asleep soon. I'm right here. Nothing is going to hurt you. If you get scared again just hold onto me."

Lauren's breathing returned to normal and she was able to go back to sleep but not before several minutes thinking about the day of the fire and what she'd do if her children were ever once again put in harm's way.

"I'm going to talk to Lauren," Beth said. "I can't sit idly by and do nothing."

Gabriel looked up from the jigsaw and lifted his safety glasses to the top of his head.

"Are you listening to me?" she asked her husband.

He then pulled his headphones off his head.

"What?"

Beth rolled her eyes. "I said that I can't sit around waiting for Lauren to ask for help. I'm going over there and talk to her."

"Okay. Can you pass me those dowels over there?"

Frustrated, Beth took the small wooden pegs in her hand and carried them to Gabriel.

"Is that all you're going to say?" she asked.

Gabriel shrugged. "What do you want me to say?"

She paused for a minute before answering him.

"I don't know, maybe try to talk me out of it," she said.

"Why exactly would I do that?"

She sat on the chair and looked at their dog Charlie. "I understand now why you go off and do your own thing, pup. Your dad is impossible."

"Charlie loves me so whatever you tell him he'll take my side," Gabriel teased.

Pouting, Beth waited for Gabriel to join her on the sofa.

"Okay, you've got my full attention. What is going on with you?"

She shrugged. "I don't know. I think it's because my sister never asks me for help."

Gabriel looked confused. "I don't understand."

"Christopher and I are super close. When he lost his leg and didn't want to live, I flew to Captiva and basically got him out of bed and on the road to recovery, both physically and emotionally. When Michael suffered from the trauma of getting shot and almost died, he told me that even though I'm his little sister, he found strength watching me and learning how I tackle life's issues. He made me feel as if I'd helped him somehow."

"Ah, I get it now. Lauren isn't coming to you for help like your brothers did. Do I have that right?"

"Is that so bad?" she asked.

"Well, it's a little selfish actually."

"Selfish? How is wanting to help people selfish?"

"Listen, I know how much you want to help Lauren, and I also know that you went into law to right the wrongs of your immediate world. But sometimes, people prefer to be left alone to deal with their issues. Lauren isn't Christopher or Michael, and you have to respect that. It's not about you, it's about Lauren and what she needs."

"Lauren doesn't know what she needs," Beth responded.

"And you do?"

That question silenced her. She shook her head. "Not really, but shouldn't I give her a chance to tell me what she needs? At the very least it would show her that I do care."

"She knows you care, honey. But, sure, either call her or go see her, just remember what we've talked about. Give her whatever space she needs."

"I'm going to use her new office space as my excuse for visiting. I'll tell her that I wanted to see the place and to see how she's doing. I can offer to be there for her if she needs me and leave it at that."

"I think that's a great idea, just remember that whatever her answer, you'll need to abide by her decisions. If she wants to be alone, then leave her alone."

Beth nodded. She understood what Gabriel was saying, but he never experienced what it was like growing up in her family. Some might say her siblings' hovering was interfering at best and downright intrusive but Beth knew better. Her family was as close as any could be, and if one member struggled, they all struggled.

It was, after all, the reason her mother invented the Code Red family alarm system, and why Beth would heed Gabriel's words by about eighty percent. The other twenty would account for the usual Wheeler family meddling tactics, and it was all in the name of love.

CHAPTER 17

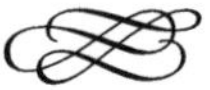

"Grandma is everything all right?" Lauren asked.

"I'm fine, what's the fuss?"

"Your text made it sound like something awful had happened."

"Oh, honey, I'm sorry. I didn't mean to scare you. I just needed to talk for a bit if you've got the time."

Lauren didn't have the time to be honest, but soon her grandmother would leave for Florida, and therefore they had little time left to spend together.

"Of course I've got the time," she lied.

Lauren looked around the living room and sighed. Although happy another young family would fill the house with the same love and laughter she'd experienced, she was sad to see it go.

It seemed that her grandmother sensed Lauren's concern.

"The place sure is empty, isn't it?"

Lauren nodded. "I'm going to miss this house."

"Well, we've got lots of memories to hold on to. How are you feeling these days? The baby must be kicking now."

Lauren smiled. "He's just started."

"He? I thought you were waiting to find out the sex of the baby."

"We are, it's just a feeling and so I keep saying 'he'."

"Lauren, I wanted to talk to you about something but I feel bad for imposing."

"What is it Grandma?"

"I'm feeling a little nervous about the move."

"What are you nervous about?"

"I hate going to the closing alone, and your mother is busy with her lunch-bunch friends. I'm going to have to deal with the movers when the truck comes…and well, I was wondering if you might come with me. It would only be for a few days, and it would help me so much having you there to organize the whole thing."

"Don't worry about a thing. Of course I'll help you move. You should have said something earlier."

"You've had a lot on your plate lately, I didn't want to bother you."

"Nonsense," Lauren said. "You could never bother me. I'm happy to do it. I've got to change a few things on my calendar and talk to Nell and Brian, but otherwise I'm all yours."

Grandma hugged Lauren. "Thank you, dear. I'm feeling much better about the whole thing."

"Have you made your airplane reservations yet?" Lauren asked.

"Yes, let me get the information so maybe we can sit together on the plane."

Grandma Sarah searched inside her purse and handed the ticket to Lauren.

"I've got to teach you how to do this with your cellphone in the future," Lauren said.

"For heaven's sake, why? I'm perfectly happy with the paper ticket Brea printed out for me."

Lauren made a note on her cellphone and then handed the ticket back to her grandmother.

"Here you go. I'll book my flight as soon as I get back to the office."

Lauren spent the next hour reminiscing with her grandmother about celebrating birthdays and holidays at her grandparents' house. Her grandfather's storytelling, and the multitude of times Lauren would walk to their home when she'd have a fight with her mother.

"I don't ever remember you taking Mom's side."

"Well, you were a teenager and everything seemed overblown to your mother."

"But, not you," Lauren said. "You always understood me better than anyone."

Her grandmother seemed to hesitate before saying more, but when she spoke her words hit Lauren hard.

"And, now? Do you still think that?"

Lauren looked out the window and didn't answer. Her focus was on keeping her composure and not letting her grandmother see her tears.

She took one last look around the room, hugged her grandmother once more and then walked to the front door. "I'd better get going. If I'm flying to Florida in a few days, I've got lots to do. Call me if you need me to do anything before we go."

Grandma Sarah nodded. "Will do. I'll talk to you soon. Be careful driving."

Her grandmother shut the door and Lauren took a deep breath before getting into her car.

Keep it together, girl. You can do this.

Feeling that her grandmother was about to ask more questions, Lauren practically ran out of the house. The thought of spending several hours traveling with her in a few days terrified Lauren.

She was able to avoid any awkwardness this time, but there

was no way Lauren could handle an interrogation that was sure to come.

Thinking about the trip as she drove to her new office, Lauren called Jeff on speaker phone.

"Hey, honey. What's up?" Jeff asked.

"My grandmother wants me to go with her to Florida to help her get settled. I'll have to talk to Nell and Brian but I thought I'd see how you felt about the situation first."

"I think it's a great idea. You need a little time in the sun. You should relax on the beach while you're there. How long will you be gone?"

"Oh, no more than a few days...a week at the most."

"I didn't mention this before because we had so much going on, but Peter's home is about to shut down. I'm going to have to help find him a new place. I'll be busy with that and the girls, so this is a perfect time for you to help your grandmother. Since the fire Michael and Brea have been great at helping out. I'll connect with them if I need anything."

"That's perfect. I'm sorry to hear about Peter though. How can they do that? Don't they realize these guys need a safe and supportive environment? You can't just separate them from each other and their seven staff members who are like family and put them anywhere."

"I know. As usual, it's a money problem. They're closing a few of these homes in the state. I'm not sure what other states are doing, but I assume it's a state budget thing. I just want to be involved with where he goes next. Our family should have a say in the matter."

"Absolutely. Well, I've got to get to the office. I'll see you at home tonight. Love you."

"Love you, too, honey."

Since Matteo's wife died, the world that he'd known for over fifty years ceased to exist. Everything changed for him. The coffee that was always brewing first thing in the morning sat quiet. The constant hum of the sewing machine throughout the day was gone. But the hardest of all was feeling the empty space in their bed where his wife slept.

For the last eighteen months, part of his new ritual was placing her nightgown in her spot. He'd get into the bed, turn on his side and place his hand on the cotton fabric. He'd even chuckle at the memory of her teasing that if he wanted a fancy lace and silk pajama wife, he'd have to look elsewhere.

He never wanted to look elsewhere, not even for one second after they'd met. He was a waiter in a coffee shop near Northeastern University and she was a student. His family never had money to send him to college but he was an exceptional, straight-A student with a photographic memory.

He charmed her into going out with him the first day they met and they were never apart for longer than a day after that.

Within months they were married. With little money to their name, the two rented a small apartment on the second floor of a three-family home in Watertown, Massachusetts.

Matteo took odd jobs here and there but his job as a plumbing apprentice was where he thrived. He worked hard to learn every aspect of the job and then, when he felt his confidence growing, he went out on his own.

Louise was a school teacher right out of college. Passionate about working with children she was fortunate to get a full-time job teaching English at the local high school.

Struggling to get pregnant, they chose traveling as much as they could to take the stress and pressure off their fertility challenges. Then, one day the miracle happened. They welcomed a daughter and named her Gia Louise, and their little family was the center of their lives.

With the baby's arrival, traveling took a backseat for several years but after a while Matteo insisted that they show Gia as much of the world as possible.

They filled photo albums with pictures of the three of them standing in front of the Eiffel Tower, the Colosseum, and the wide expanse of green hills and valleys in Switzerland.

They weren't rich by any means. They worked hard and saved their money, finding the best deals through their travel agency each time. They wanted to expose Gia to as much as possible so that when she grew up and had a family of her own she would share her experiences and knowledge with them.

Except for the Dakotas, there wasn't a state in the US that they hadn't visited. Over the years, the Benedettis covered more geography than most people in several lifetimes. Whenever anyone criticized them for not staying home more, Matteo would explain to people that his wife being a teacher, as well as their family adventures, taught Gia more than any classroom could.

Sitting under the Key Lime Garden Inn's gazebo, Matteo looked back over his life and smiled. He had been lucky to be married to the most amazing woman and for that he was immensely grateful.

When Paolo Moretti was finished mowing the lawn, he approached Matteo.

"Good afternoon, Matteo," Paolo said.

"Another beautiful Captiva day, Mr. Moretti."

Paolo took a cloth from his back pocket and wiped the perspiration from the back of his neck.

"We're headed into the Florida summer heat. You're probably not used to this. Didn't you say you live in Minnesota?"

Matteo shook his head. "I was born in Minnesota, but my family came east when I was about thirteen."

"Any siblings?" Paolo asked.

"Yes, I have one brother. He's older than me by a couple of years. He lives in Bonita Springs now."

Paolo looked confused. "I'm sorry, I thought you lived in colder weather. We've had so many guests over the years I think I'm getting people mixed up."

Matteo laughed. "Understandable."

He didn't want to explain that he'd become used to Florida summers by now, or that he'd been living in Bonita Springs the last...well, many years now.

He'd already skirted the important questions, he couldn't address the harder ones...the more personal questions.

He rose from his chair and leaned on his cane. "I think I'll go inside and enjoy some of your very nice air conditioning."

Paolo laughed. "We've got plenty of that and thank heaven that we do. You have a nice day, Matteo."

Matteo waved and walked toward the inn. He was very tired. Tired of feeling weaker by the day, but mostly tired of reliving a life that had long been gone. He'd spent the last two hours reminiscing and it felt more like watching a movie on someone else's life. In his mind, he'd already moved on. Soon, he would leave the past behind and his wife would be waiting with open arms.

CHAPTER 18

Between the speech therapist, occupational therapist and Jacqui Hutchins, Devon's health improved each day. His recovery was slow and would still take months before there could be any discussion about his returning to work. However, with his limited speech and constant stuttering, Devon was able to communicate his position on issues impacting both family and business.

"Can I take it that you're pleased with how we're handling things?" Trevor asked his father.

Devon nodded. "I…am. How…is Wyatt…doing?"

Trevor laughed. "He stopped fighting Clayton and me, so that's a good thing. Seriously, he seems to be managing. I knew that Wyatt was smart, but his stubbornness always got in the way. He's run several of our tours on the new development and is even handling the PR, all the while reaching out to both the community and small real estate firms. He's surprising all of us in the office."

Jacqui rubbed her father's shoulder. "See, Dad? Everything is working out, and just as soon as you can get yourself out of this wheelchair without assistance, you'll be running things at work once again."

Eliza came into the room and turned the blinds. "I can't wait for that day. He's been barking orders...well, his version of barking, ever since he found his voice again. He needs to start bossing his employees around instead of me and the maid."

Devon made a face at his wife, and both Jacqui and Trevor smiled, enjoying their father's return to his usual teasing of their mother.

"I think the important thing is that, at least for the time being, we're all getting along. If you were to ask me two months ago if that would ever happen, I would have thought you crazy for even suggesting it."

Devon nodded. "I...want...to see him."

Trevor didn't know what to say. For all his brother's attempts to make peace with him and Clayton, he stayed away from visiting their father. Trevor never brought the subject up and let it slide given that Wyatt kept his head down and did his job.

"He's been very busy, Dad. I'm sure he'll come by soon."

Eliza looked at Trevor and shook her head. Trevor felt he'd told a lie but had no other solution.

Distracting her father, Jacqui said, "Dad, let's try to play checkers again. This time, I'm going to win."

Trevor felt awful. It was unreasonable to expect Wyatt and their father to mend ways overnight, but he thought at the very least his brother could pretend to care about Devon's health.

Jacqui set up the checkers board and pulled a chair across from Devon. They began playing while Trevor and Eliza quietly slipped out of the room.

"You've got to talk to your brother," Eliza whispered. "He can't stay away forever."

Trevor nodded. "I know. I'll see what I can do."

"What if he won't cooperate?" she asked.

"I'll have to come up with a good enough reason for him to see Dad."

"I don't care what you offer him, just get him here, and soon."

By nine o'clock each morning, Millie would see Matteo either walking around the inn's property, or heading toward the street, but not this morning.

She finished mopping the floor in the kitchen and then looked for Maggie.

"Have you seen Mr. Benedetti this morning?" she asked.

"Not today, but then again, I was with Paolo in the garden for the last hour. Why? Do you need him for something?" Maggie asked.

"No, it's just that I'm used to seeing him, and well…"

"You're worried about him, aren't you?"

Millie nodded. "I am. He's been looking awfully weak and pale."

Maggie put the basket of apples down on the kitchen island. "I think we're all worried about him."

Riley looked up from the sink. "He usually takes a walk around the property, and always stops to wave at me, but I didn't see him this morning and he didn't come to the dining room for breakfast."

"I noticed the door to his room is closed. Do you think I should check on him?" Millie asked.

Maggie shook her head. "No. I think he probably left the inn early and went somewhere. It's not for us to track down the movements of our guests. He has a right to go where he wants, whenever he wants. I'm sure he's fine."

Millie wasn't convinced but didn't want to anger Maggie. She had to do what her boss instructed and that would have to be the end of it.

By two o'clock, when no one had seen him, Millie searched for Maggie once again to get permission to enter the room. When Maggie finally gave her the go-ahead, Millie gently knocked on Mr. Benedetti's bedroom door.

His voice faint, he answered her. "Come in."

Leaving his door open, she went inside and found him still in his bed.

"Mr. Benedetti, are you all right?"

He tried to pull himself up to lean against the headboard but seemed unable to do so.

"Let me help you."

Putting her arms under his, she lifted him up and settled him in place.

"Thank you, Millie. I wasn't feeling well this morning and thought I'd use the day to stay in bed. Have you ever had a day like that?"

She smiled. "Of course, but I call them mental health days."

Matteo laughed. "That's a good one. Let's call today a mental health day then. Why don't you pull up a chair and sit with me? I could use a distraction."

"I'm happy to spend some time with you, but first I think we should get you something to eat and drink. You must be hungry."

"I wasn't this morning, but I think I could take some food now," he said.

"How does a bowl of soup sound? Riley has a pot on the stove."

"That would be lovely, thank you."

Millie ran to the kitchen and informed Maggie, Riley and Iris of Mr. Benedetti's situation.

"Millie, you let us know if he needs a doctor. I can get someone over here in fifteen minutes if he does."

Millie nodded. "I will. He wants me to sit with him for a bit. I'll get this soup in him and let you know if he gets worse."

Millie brought the soup to Matteo, sat next to him and slowly spoon-fed him until he'd had a few bites.

"You had us worried when we didn't see you this morning. Do you feel that you need a doctor? We have one that lives nearby."

He shook his head. "No. I'm not that sick. I just needed a day to rest. My leg sometimes gives me trouble and I have to get off it for several hours. That usually helps."

Millie was certain that Matteo's illness was more serious than a painful leg. "So, it's your leg, then, that's giving you trouble? Nothing else?"

He smiled. "Nothing to worry about. Now, tell me what's been going on in your life these days? You can't always be working. What do you do when you're not cleaning and organizing the Key Lime Garden Inn?"

She fed him more of the soup before answering him.

"Well, I live in Ft. Myers for now. I hope eventually to buy something here on Captiva, or maybe even Sanibel. It's expensive on the island so it's going to take time."

"Do you have a husband or children?"

Millie shook her head. "Oh no, it's just me. I was married and lived in Maine, but I'm divorced now and happily living in Florida. The Morettis and everyone here at the inn are my family."

"You're very lucky to have them. Everyone needs a family. How long have you lived in Florida?"

"About nine months. My mother used to work here too, but that was a long time ago. She was a domestic worker before I was born. She's gone now, though. I do miss her."

"My goodness, you're a legacy."

Millie laughed. "Yes, I guess I am."

"Do you think you'll be working here ten years from now?"

Her brow furrowed. "That's a strange question. What makes you ask that?"

"I just wondered if this is where you plan to settle and live out your life or if this is just a stop along the way to someplace else."

Millie shrugged. "I'm not so sure. I guess I never thought about it like that before. Do you have a magic crystal ball? What does my future look like?"

He looked into her eyes and smiled. "I predict this is where you will build a wonderful life. Do you know why I think that?"

Millie shook her head.

"Because, Millie, I think it took you a very long time to get here. You didn't just happen to find your way to Captiva. Your mother lived here and loved it, and that's why you're here. You found your mother in the sunsets, the palm trees and tourists. She's in the sand, the ocean, the tropical drinks and seashells. You're connected to Captiva just like I am."

Millie sat mesmerized by his words. She couldn't understand how a stranger who knew nothing about her could so completely reach into her heart and speak about her dreams before she knew them herself.

Her voice just a whisper, she asked him, "How are you connected to Captiva, Mr. Benedetti?"

He didn't answer her, instead reaching for the bowl of soup. "Do you think there's more of this in the kitchen?"

"Of course. I'll go get some. Would you like anything else?"

"Maybe a piece of bread to go with it?"

She nodded. "Be right back."

"He'd like a piece of bread with more soup," Millie said to Riley.

"I just pulled my sourdough out of the oven. Let me cut a piece," Iris said.

Millie looked at Maggie. "I asked him but he said he doesn't need a doctor. He said his leg is what's giving him trouble and that he'll be fine tomorrow if he spends today resting."

"He must be feeling better," Maggie said. "Are you all right, Millie? You look like you've seen a ghost."

"I'm fine. It's just...there's something about him."

"Mr. Benedetti?" Maggie asked.

Millie nodded but couldn't explain her feelings.

Riley smiled. "You think so, too?"

Maggie looked at Riley. "What do you mean?"

"Well, the other day I was feeling kind of down. I can't even explain it, but somehow Mr. Benedetti sensed it and took the time to talk to me. By the time our conversation was over, I felt wonderful...even euphoric."

"I'd better get back before he thinks we're all out here talking about him," Millie said.

"You mean like we are?" Maggie teased.

"Exactly."

When she went back to his room, Mr. Benedetti's eyes were closed and he appeared to be sleeping. Instead of leaving the soup and bread, Millie turned and tiptoed out of the room, closing the door behind her.

CHAPTER 19

All the scuttle and activity around the Key Lime Garden Inn was more chaotic than usual. With Maggie and Chelsea's lunch-bunch ladies arriving in the afternoon, everyone was up early to prepare for their arrival. Even Chelsea found her way to the inn to see if Maggie needed an extra pair of hands.

Caught in the kitchen munching on a cranberry and walnut scone, Chelsea looked guilty.

Standing in front of Chelsea with her hands on her hips, Maggie complained, "I thought you were here to help?"

"I am but I need energy don't I? I'm getting it in the form of your delicious scones and caffeine," Chelsea explained. "What do you need me to do?"

Maggie sat at the kitchen table across from Chelsea and watched her friend eat. "You're taller than me, so maybe you can help Paolo with the decorations in the living room."

"Decorations?"

"Sarah insisted that we should have a welcome banner, a congratulations banner, and twinkling white lights strung around here and there. Paolo's already started."

"What time are they getting here?"

"They took the six am flight out of Logan so I expect they'll be here before noon. As usual they've ordered a van so they can drive here together."

"Did you talk to Diana about bringing her cookbook?" Maggie asked.

"I did. She's a bit confused why we're asking her to bring it along on her vacation. I explained that we want to encourage her to publish it."

"How did she sound?"

"I'm concerned about her. Diana used to be so upbeat and excited about everything. This isn't like her at all."

Maggie sighed. "I really hope we can get her to snap out of it. Not just for Jane's sake, but for her own. She can't continue like this."

"Speaking of being down in the dumps, how is Lauren these days?"

Maggie shrugged. "I'm not sure. I talked to my mother about her, and Beth too. They're all doing their best to help her but I think she needs professional help. It kills me that I can't be with her, but I'm not sure what I can say or do that would make a difference."

Chelsea reached for Maggie's hand. "Just love her and be there for her. I'm guessing that in time she'll come to you. You and your family are the medicine all that girl needs. I'm not saying that professional help isn't needed, but the closeness and love that you all have for one another usually is enough to heal every broken heart and spirit."

"Thank you, Chelsea, that's really sweet of you to say. I hope you're right. Every member of my family is working to help Lauren in any way they can."

Paolo came into the kitchen with a string of tangled lights. "I don't think I ever learn. I put these back after Christmas and now they don't work and I'm sure it's because one light is out but there's no way I can find it."

Just then Sarah walked into the kitchen carrying a clipboard. "I've checked off about four things, but there's still plenty to do."

She looked at Paolo and laughed. "It's okay, Paolo. I think we can skip the twinkling lights."

Paolo's relieved sigh made Maggie laugh. "Honey, do you need help with the banners?"

"I'm done with those and ready to head over to Sanibellia unless you ladies need me for anything else?"

"Nope. We're good. Thanks, Paolo," Sarah said.

Paolo kissed Maggie and went out the back door to the car.

"He couldn't get out of here fast enough," Chelsea said.

Laughing, Maggie said, "Wait until the lunch-bunch crew shows up. We won't see Paolo for days."

"Well, I'm headed home to put my bathing suit on. I expect we'll all spend the day at the beach. The last time they were here it was the first thing they wanted to do."

Maggie nodded. "It's so hot out, I have no doubt they'll want to jump into the water right away."

"I'm headed home but I'll be back later today to say hello to everyone. Have fun this afternoon, but don't forget to be showered and dressed by six-thirty. You all have reservations at The Bubble Room at seven," Sarah added.

"Yes, Mother," Maggie teased.

Chelsea laughed. "What do I always say? Sarah gets more like you by the day."

"Don't you have to go home and get ready?" Maggie asked.

"I'm going," Chelsea answered while stealing a scone on her way out the door.

Maggie and Chelsea set up lounge chairs, umbrellas and a small table with lemonade and iced tea where the inn's beach path meets the sand. Riley prepared two baskets of sandwiches and fruit along with chips and salsa.

"This looks like we're staying for a few days. How much food do you think we're going to eat?" Chelsea asked.

"You know what travel day is like," Maggie answered. "Airplane food is never that good. I'm always starving and looking for the nearest restaurant when I get off a plane."

Chelsea sighed. "Well, you certainly took care of that. I'm just hoping we all have appetites when we get to The Bubble Room for dinner. I absolutely have to have one of their cakes, and we know how big those things are."

"Let's leave this for now. The girls should be arriving any minute," Maggie said.

By the time they reached the porch, the van carrying their friends was pulling up in front of the carriage house.

Jane was the first one out of the van, followed by Kelly, Rachel, and Diana.

"Yay! You made it!" Maggie said, running to them and throwing her arms around them one-by-one, with Chelsea not far behind.

"That flight is so short, I don't know why we don't fly down here more often," Jane said.

"Because you're usually gallivanting around the country for work," Kelly answered.

"True, but that's going to change. I'm slowing down now that I'm getting married."

"She means now that she's engaged to a billionaire," Chelsea added.

"Oh stop. He's not that rich...well, maybe." Jane winked.

Maggie didn't think it possible but Diana looked worse in person than she did on video.

"Maggie and I have set up all kinds of goodies on the beach. Why don't you all get inside and change into your bathing suits and we'll spend the afternoon relaxing and planning the next few days?" Chelsea said.

"I love that we get the inn all to ourselves," Rachel said.

"Well, almost. We do have one gentleman staying in the first floor bedroom. He's very quiet and won't bother you at all during your stay."

"Bother us?" Jane asked. "More like we'll bother him. I hope he knows we can get a little loud."

Maggie looked at Chelsea. "I've told him. He goes about his business and won't care what we do. If you do run into him, his name is Mr. Benedetti...Matteo."

Jane looked at Chelsea and smiled. "Is he single?"

"Don't go there, Jane. He's a recent widower, and not very well, but thanks for thinking of me."

Maggie rolled her eyes at Jane's comment. She'd long ago believed that Jane would never marry and would remain single for the rest of her life.

Jane had never been a proponent of marriage and made that fact known to all. Until recently, she stood out in the group as the one who cherished her freedom, often dating multiple men simultaneously.

The announcement of her engagement came as a total surprise to the group, especially Maggie, who harbored doubts about the longevity of Jane's marriage with her betrothed.

Despite her reservations, Maggie decided to celebrate the occasion with her best friends and agreed to host the bachelorette party at the inn. She could think of no place better than Captiva as the ideal setting for them to unwind and gossip under the hot Florida sun.

Once everyone was settled in their rooms, they got changed and met Chelsea and Maggie outside.

Nodding in the direction of the gazebo, Diana asked, "Is that your guest sitting over there?"

Maggie waved at Matteo who waved back. "That's him. Matteo Benedetti. He's a lovely man."

Although Matteo smiled, his sadness was still evident, and Diana was the first to notice it.

"How long has it been since his wife died?"

"Less than two years. I think Paolo said eighteen months."

The ladies continued to the beach and Maggie noticed that Diana stayed behind everyone else and waved to Matteo before catching up to the group. Maggie smiled, thinking that if Diana could find a kindred spirit in Matteo then the bachelorette party would be worth every minute of time spent to make it happen.

"Okay, ladies, we've finally arrived in heaven," Jane said while twirling on the sand. "Feel that sun, isn't it amazing."

"It's pretty amazing," Rachel said. "What do you think, Kelly? Is this amazing or what?"

Kelly nodded. "I think you're right, Rachel. It's very amazing."

"Okay, okay, I get it. Make fun of me all you want, but I'm dancing on a cloud over here."

Jane pulled her cover-up off and challenged everyone to a swim. "Last one in is a rotten egg," she yelled as she ran toward the water.

"Is it me, or is she trying too hard?" Diana said.

"Meaning?" Maggie asked.

Diana shrugged. "I don't know, it's just that I'm not so convinced that everything is as wonderful as she's made it out to be."

"You think something's wrong between her and what's-his-name?" Chelsea asked.

"Brian," said Rachel, Kelly and Diana in unison.

"And, yes, I do," Diana added. "I hate to be a downer here, and I realize this would be considered bad form during a bachelorette party, but I'd bet money that the wedding doesn't happen."

"Diana!" Rachel yelled. "Don't say that."

Kelly stayed quiet on the subject, but she didn't dispute Diana's prediction either.

"If something is going on between them, Jane will spill before this week is over. I don't think she'll be able to put on a happy face several days in a row," Chelsea said. "I think we all have to be supportive and, when the time is right, she'll tell us what's really going on."

"She'd better," Diana said. "The wedding is only four months away."

Their happy mood was already starting to change and Maggie needed to do something to get them back in celebratory mode.

"I have a thought. What if you're all wrong about this and there's nothing to worry about? Instead of enjoying this beautiful place, we're sitting here complaining about something that might never happen."

"Maggie's right. I've missed you guys and now that we're here together again I want us to have a good time," Chelsea said. "Let's get in the water and talk about our plans for the week."

Maggie wanted to hug Chelsea for her support and encouragement. Whatever was going on with Jane would reveal itself in time.

In the meantime, even if Jane and Brian never made it to the altar, her closest friends were on Captiva Island making new memories they'd talk about for years to come.

CHAPTER 20

Ciara needed support and Sarah was just the person to help. She found the perfect dress for her wedding and now, all she needed to do was convince her Maid of Honor to make the trip to Italy.

Holding her dress up for Sarah to see, Ciara beamed. "Don't you just love it? I saw it in the window and that was that."

Sarah clapped her hands. "It's beautiful, Ciara. I wish we could have found your dress when we went shopping. I would have loved watching you try on a bunch of dresses while sipping champagne."

"If I'm not mistaken, we have a bottle in the refrigerator," Trevor said as he walked into the room. "I'll pour the champagne but then I'm out of here. I don't need to talk about dresses with you two."

"Thanks, hon, but I think you should join us."

"I'm happy to open a bottle for you ladies, but then I'm going to take the kids to the park for a little while before I have to go into the office," Trevor answered.

"Actually Trevor, I'm glad that you're here. I was hoping you could help me convince your wife to be in my wedding. She's stubborn and won't go to Italy without you."

Sarah looked at Trevor and then back at Ciara and pouted. "I've tried to talk him into going to Italy, but he thinks the office will fall apart if he's not there."

Trevor popped the cork on the champagne bottle and smiled. "That's how much you know," he said. "I have a meeting with Wyatt and Clayton this afternoon to talk about me going to Italy."

Their faces lit up at Trevor's words as he held up his hand. "Hold on. Before you two book our flight, you need to understand that if I don't feel comfortable with leaving, I'm not going."

"I understand, "Sarah said.

"Listen to me, Sarah. Regardless, I really want you to go. I can call Debbie and see if she'll adjust her hours to be a full-time nanny while you're away. This is a once in a lifetime event, and I know Ciara would appreciate it so much."

Ciara nodded. "He's right. You've already got the dress. My wedding won't be the same without you in it. Please come," she pleaded.

Sarah sighed and then nodded her head in agreement. "I'm in."

"Yes!" Ciara yelled, and then threw her arms around Sarah. "Thank you so much, Sarah. I mean it. We're going to have so much fun."

Trevor hugged Sarah and handed her and Ciara each a glass of champagne. "I've got to get the kids ready."

"Okay, honey. I'll see you before you go to the office."

Sarah grabbed Ciara's arm and pulled her into the front room.

"What?" Ciara asked.

"I didn't want Trevor to hear us talking but I'm so excited that he might join us in Italy. I hope Wyatt comes through for him. In the meantime, I just got a call from my friend Emma Thurston."

"Oh, right. That's Jillian's sister. Jillian and Joshua will be at the wedding," Ciara said.

Sarah nodded. “Exactly. She said that if we do go to Italy, she and Gareth will meet us there.”

“That’s exciting, but why is this a secret from Trevor?”

“Because Trevor isn’t a huge fan of Gareth’s and I don’t want to say anything that might keep him from agreeing to go with me. You know how stubborn he can be. Even if Wyatt cooperates, Trevor could still use the office as an excuse if he wanted a good enough reason to get out of going. I’m not going to give him that opportunity.”

Ciara chuckled, “Smart girl.”

Sarah took another sip of her champagne. “Well, I do know my husband.”

“Do we need the conference room?” Clayton asked Trevor.

“No, we can meet in my office if that works for everyone.”

“I’ve got a meeting at four o’clock across town so I hope this won’t take long,” Clayton said.

“Now who’s slacking off?” Wyatt said as he entered the room. “Everyone knows you leave the office by three to go see your new girlfriend. Why try to hide it?”

“Knock it off, Wyatt. My private life is none of your business. Not everyone’s dating life is plastered all over social media like yours.”

Trevor was losing patience with his brothers. “Can we get to why I called this meeting? I’ve got a situation that I want to run by the two of you. My father-in-law’s sister Ciara is getting married in Italy and Sarah is the Maid of Honor. I’d like to accompany my wife to Italy and I’m seriously thinking of making it a family vacation by bringing the kids with us. I know we’ve got a lot on our schedules right now, and it’s probably not the best time to take a vacation, but it can’t be helped.”

"And you want to know if Clayton and I can handle the workload while you're gone?" Wyatt asked.

Trevor nodded. "Yes. Some things can be put off for a week or so, but there are a few things that can't be overlooked. The construction schedule is what it is and my leaving won't change that."

"I don't see any problem with you going. Are you talking for a week?" Clayton asked.

"More like ten days. We're running out of time. The wedding is nine days from today. We've got to plan for after the wedding. I'd like for the family to see as many sites as we can. Probably the big cities of Rome, Venice and Florence."

"Where's the wedding?" Wyatt asked.

"A seaside town called Gaeta. I had to look on the map to see where it is."

"I've been there," Wyatt said. "It's a beautiful place."

Trevor laughed. "Of course you have. Where haven't you been?"

Wyatt's face turned serious. "I expect to see more places soon. I miss traveling."

Trevor got Wyatt's meaning. It was a not-so-veiled attempt at letting Trevor and Clayton know his future plans. As frustrated as Trevor was to think about how his family, especially Devon, would react to this news, he saved discussing that topic for another time.

"So, what do you guys think? Can you cover for me?"

"Take your family to Italy and enjoy yourself, brother," Wyatt answered.

Clayton agreed with Wyatt.

"We'll be fine here. We should look at the calendars and Wyatt and I will take on whatever we have to. I'll have my assistant work on making calls where necessary."

"Thanks, guys. I really mean it. Sarah and I both appreciate your understanding."

Clayton rose from his chair. "I've got to go. I'll catch up with you guys later."

As he walked toward the door, Wyatt yelled at him, "Say hello to your girlfriend from me. Give her my cellphone number and tell her if things don't work out with you..."

Trevor shook his head. "Will you ever stop?"

Wyatt got up and started to leave before Trevor stopped him. "Wait. I'm glad that Clayton is gone because I wanted to talk to you about something."

Trevor motioned to the sofa. "Let's sit down."

"Oh, this can't be good. Brother dear needs me to sit down. Sounds like a lecture is coming."

Wyatt sat on the sofa.

"Do you want something to drink?"

"Just get to the point, Trevor."

Trevor nodded. "Okay. I'll get right to it. Why aren't you seeing Dad? Spare me the history lesson. I've been there. I know what our past looks like and I know what's going on now, but for the life of me, I don't understand why you can't be a man and let the past go."

Wyatt laughed. "You're really something, you know that? You think your perception of our family history is the same as mine."

"I never said that...it's just that..."

Wyatt finished Trevor's sentence, "It's just that you haven't a clue how I feel about things. To this day, you think I'm upset with our Dad because he was mean to me. You don't get what it's like to constantly try to gain his love only to watch him give it to you."

Trevor shook his head. "This is textbook stuff. I'm not getting blamed for what Dad did or didn't do. Or, better yet, your perception of what Dad did or didn't do. Maybe it's time you talk to him and find out once and for all what he thinks about you?"

"I have no desire to..."

"To what? Get to the truth so that maybe, just maybe, you'll have to give up the lie you've been telling yourself all these years? Because you and I both know that to do that might mean that you'll have to see Dad in a different light. You won't be able to continue playing the victim…the wronged son."

His face red and his body stiff, Wyatt seemed unable to speak, and Trevor knew why.

"You think Dad doesn't care about you, but you're wrong. He loves you."

Wyatt shot up off the sofa and stormed toward the door but stopped when Trevor yelled to him.

"Dad has been asking for you."

Wyatt turned and looked at Trevor.

Trevor continued. "I go to see him every day, and every day he asks for you. The man can barely speak, and yet, your name is the first word out of his mouth. Does that sound like someone who doesn't love you?"

Wyatt looked as if he was going to cry. Instead, he swallowed and shook his head. "I can't. Don't ask me to. I just can't."

Trevor felt Wyatt's pain. Trevor had been separated from their father for years, but nothing between them was as fraught with such internal conflict and trauma. It was more than Wyatt could do to stand in front of Trevor like this. His body trembling from a deep emotional struggle that wouldn't let go of the pain.

The unresolved issues that lingered between father and son were familiar to Trevor, but his own experience wasn't enough to reach his brother.

Their fractured family would continue indefinitely unless Wyatt changed his mind. Devon wouldn't, or more accurately, couldn't, and all Trevor could do was pray that in time, something would soften Wyatt's heart.

"Do what you have to, Wyatt, but know this. Whenever you're ready to mend things with Dad, I'll be right beside you, supporting you all the way."

Wyatt nodded and seemed grateful that Trevor was in his

corner. Trevor watched his brother walk out of his office and reminded himself to not judge.

Wyatt was right about one thing. Their journeys, although similar, were not the same at all. Trevor would need to remind himself not to judge but instead to be patient with his brother.

The road ahead was long but Trevor could see a light at the end of the tunnel. Something that hadn't been there for a very long time.

CHAPTER 21

The Bubble Room was Captiva Island's most popular restaurant and tourist attraction. The food was great and the desserts spectacular. But it was the decor that had everyone pulling out their cellphones to take pictures.

From The Bubble Room Gorilla Cage outside to the Tunnel of Love inside, the colorful rooms filled with nostalgia was everyone's favorite place to gather.

"I'm having The Golden Age of Hollywood. It looks delish," Jane said.

"That has tequila in it. I haven't had tequila in I don't know how long," Chelsea said.

"It's not that wild. It's basically a Margarita," Maggie added. "I'm going for the Put the Lime in the Coconut."

"Oh, I've had that one before. I'll join you," Chelsea said.

By the time their table was ready, the women each had their tropical drink in hand. Their host sat them at a table that had a glass cover over several old Hollywood celebrity photos underneath.

Pointing to one photo, Kelly said, "Look, there's Marilyn Monroe, oh and Gene Kelly, and Mickey Rooney."

"I love this place. Every time we come here I think of my childhood," Maggie said.

"Your childhood? You mean you watched a bunch of old movies when you were a kid?" Chelsea asked.

"No. Not that. I mean the movie star photos are cool, but I love all the old toys they have here. Did you see the model trains overhead in the bar? My dad always put together a train set to run around the Christmas tree every year."

"Oh, my dad did that too," said Diana. "Christmas was always so wonderful growing up."

A tinge of sadness on Diana's face made Maggie wonder if every subject they talked about on this trip would send Diana into a depressive slump. Maggie worried that they'd run out of things to talk about at this rate.

"Let's all order our food and then I have a plan for tomorrow that I want to talk about," Maggie said.

"Ooh, that sounds mysterious," Jane said. "Whatever it is if it involves scaring me, don't do it. The last thing I want to do is ride a rollercoaster."

"Oh for heaven's sake, Jane. When was the last time this group went on a rollercoaster?" Chelsea asked. "I don't think any of us could handle more than a merry-go-round."

"You mean a carousel," Rachel corrected Chelsea.

"I meant a merry-go-round. Who calls that a carousel?"

"Everyone, everywhere," Maggie teased.

"Whatever. You get my meaning. Maybe a Ferris wheel. That would be fun," Chelsea added.

"I'm afraid of heights," Diana said.

Maggie rolled her eyes. "Guys, focus. We're not going to an amusement park."

"Oh, thank heaven," Jane said between sips of her Golden Age of Hollywood.

After they ordered their dinners, Maggie looked directly at Diana.

"As most of you don't know, our friend Diana has a significant portion of her cookbook completed. Chelsea and I asked her to bring the book here so that we all could help her get it finalized and ready for publication."

"Diana, I had no idea you've been working on a cookbook," Rachel said.

"That's fantastic, Diana, " Kelly added.

"How exactly are we going to help Diana finish this book?" Jane asked.

"That's the best part. We're all going to bake some delicious desserts tomorrow. Riley and Iris are going to help us. We've got just about every ingredient for baking. Tons of pots, pans and cookie sheets. We'll have the kitchen for the day and all the flour, sugar and butter you could ever need."

Jane looked like Maggie had stuck a pin in her balloon. "I guess it could be fun," she said.

"Maggie, you don't have to do this," Diana said, her voice as monotone as ever.

"Of course we do. Make no mistake, the book is yours, we don't want to take over, we want to help. We'll take direction from you."

Maggie looked around the table for support. "We all have recipes we can add to the book too. Maybe a lunch-bunch addendum or something. What do you all think?"

"I'm game. I think it will be fun," Kelly said.

"I'm hoping we get to eat our recipes after we photograph them?" Chelsea asked.

"Absolutely," Maggie answered.

"I've got a few recipes I can contribute," Rachel said.

"We're going to make a big mess in your kitchen Maggie," Diana said.

Maggie put her hand on Diana's. "But just think how beautiful it looks after you've cleaned up the mess. That's when you appreciate it the most."

"Doesn't Mom have her lunch-bunch friends staying at the inn this week?" Lauren asked Grandma Sarah as they loaded up the trunk with their luggage.

"Yes, I believe so, why?"

"Nothing. I was just wondering if she knew that this was the week you were moving to Florida. It just seems weird that she'd schedule her get-together the same week you're moving into your condo."

Grandma Sarah shrugged. "I'm pretty sure that we can get me settled without your mother's help. We don't need her, do we?" she asked, judging Lauren's mood.

Lauren shook her head. "No, I suppose not."

Grandma knew better. If anyone could influence Lauren, it was her mother. Maggie was the only person who, with only a pot of freshly-brewed tea, could get at the heart of her children's concerns, and Grandma was counting on it this time.

Whether she knew it or not, Lauren was about to finally share the pain she'd been dealing with ever since the fire. A nice long talk would get to the bottom of things once and for all.

"Let's get going, I want to be in the Florida heat by noon," Grandma said.

They got into Lauren's car and headed for Logan Airport, and Grandma tried not to giggle. She'd been sneaky enough to get Lauren this far, she could only hope she was clever enough to keep her granddaughter from flying back to Massachusetts before her plan could work.

The gate was packed with travelers. Grandma and Lauren found two available seats near the window.

"I've got to go to the ladies room, and I'm hungry. Can you stay here and watch our bags?" Grandma asked.

"Of course. We've got plenty of time before boarding," Lauren answered.

Grandma Sarah found a quiet spot near the ladies room, pulled her cellphone out of her purse and called Chelsea.

"Hey Sarah. How nice of you to call. Is everything all right?" Chelsea asked.

"Everything's fine. I'm at Logan Airport getting ready to fly into Ft. Myers. I've got Lauren with me."

"Oh, I didn't realize that you were coming today. I think Maggie expects you at the end of the week."

"Yes, I know that but I'm sure you've heard about what Lauren is going through."

"I'm so sorry about the fire. Maggie told me that Lauren has been having a difficult time ever since."

"Well, you and I know that the only solution for that is to get Lauren and Maggie together. She needs her mother, and the way I see it is if Maggie won't come to her, then Lauren has to go to Maggie."

"Sarah, I'm a little confused. Does Lauren want to see Maggie?"

"Well, I'm sure that she does but she's stubborn. She thinks nothing's wrong but we all know there is. Anyway, I don't have much time here. I need your help. I've told Lauren that I'm to get the keys for the condo today."

"And that's a lie?"

"Yes, they're not ready for me for another three days. I just wanted to get Lauren here as soon as possible. I'm going to pretend that I made a mistake and I can't move into the condo for another three days. Can we stay at your place? I know Maggie has her friends staying at the inn."

Chelsea laughed. "Oh, Sarah, you are a piece of work. I'll leave the front door unlocked. There is plenty of food in the fridge if you're hungry. But, let me get this straight, I'm not to breathe a word of this to Maggie?"

"That's right. It's not that we won't see her later, I just don't want her to influence the situation one way or the other. She and Lauren will have to deal with this situation face-to-face, and I'm just the person to make sure that happens."

"I understand," Chelsea answered.

"I just got tired of waiting around for them to fix this. Let's face it, Chelsea, these two women are stubborn mules. I have no idea where they ever learned such behavior."

"I've no idea," Chelsea said.

"Well, I've got to go. We might be boarding soon. We'll see you tonight then?"

"Yes, although I don't have any idea what time. Your granddaughter, Sarah, has us booked to do something tonight. No worries though. I'll catch up with you eventually. Make sure you text me if you have any questions or need anything. I'll do my best to discreetly answer."

"Thank you, Chelsea. Cross your fingers that this doesn't blow up in my face. Maggie's been known to lose patience with me. I don't know why I put up with it. Goodbye, and thanks again."

As soon as she ended the call, Grandma Sarah heard the announcement that they were boarding her plane. She took a deep breath and approached Lauren with a distressed look on her face.

"What's the matter, Grandma?"

"Oh, Lauren, you won't believe what I did. I got the date mixed up and just realized in the ladies room that we're going to Florida three days too early. I can't believe this."

Lauren didn't seem disturbed by this news. "Oh, that's all right. Don't worry, we can manage. I'll call them and see if we can get in early. It's possible the place is empty anyway. As long as no one is living there, you should be fine."

Grandma hadn't considered this possibility, and so she upped her game. Visibly shaken, she let tears form in her eyes. "No, that won't work. I don't want to get a reputation for already starting to be a headache for them right from the start. I called Chelsea. We can stay there and then arrive on the proper day."

"You called Chelsea? Why not call Mom?"

"Because dear, your mother has a house full of guests. She's already so busy I don't want to be a nuisance. It will be fine. Chelsea is leaving the front door unlocked so we'll just let ourselves in. We can stop by the inn and say hello to everyone after we've unpacked and had lunch. Now, let's go, they're calling our row.

CHAPTER 22

The truck's beeping kept everyone away from the delivery. As it backed up in front of the carriage house, Rachel came out onto the porch to join Maggie.

"What in the world is going on?" she asked.

"Paolo ordered lumber for a project he has going on at the back of our property. He's working on building a small cottage with a cabana nearer to the beach. To be honest when he mentioned it to me I didn't have his vision. I couldn't see it. But then he showed me a picture in a coastal living magazine. The photo was of a bed & breakfast in the Bahamas that had what he wanted to recreate. You should have seen this place. It was incredible."

"It sounds gorgeous," Rachel said.

Maggie nodded. "We're going to charge more for that room. Guests will walk through the flower garden and just beyond the koi pond is their private oasis."

"Sounds lovely, when can I move in?" Diana asked as she joined them on the porch.

Maggie laughed. "Anytime, sweetie. You can stay with us for as long as you want."

Jane and Kelly finally got up and shuffled half-asleep into the kitchen. Riley had breakfast ready and called everyone to the table.

"Thank heaven, I'm starving," Diana said.

Chelsea arrived just as Riley was putting the last plate on the table. "Sorry I'm late, I had a few things to take care of this morning."

"You're not late. We all just got up," Kelly said.

The screech of the screened back door slammed and got everyone's attention. Sarah, once again carrying her clipboard, made Chelsea laugh.

"Here's our cruise director coming to tell us how we're going to spend the day," she teased.

"Very funny, Chelsea. Well, today is an easy one. I had scheduled you all for a spa day, but Mom called me and said that you all planned to have a day baking pastries. If that is what you all want to do, who am I to judge?"

Jane looked less than excited about the plans.

"No worries though. I was able to reschedule you for the day after tomorrow. Tonight, you'll be guests on a sunset cruise, complete with dinner, drinks and live music."

"Now, you're talking," Jane said.

"I'm off to spend the day planning for our trip to Italy but I'll be back just before you board the cruise."

"Italy? You're going after all?" Maggie asked.

Sarah nodded. "Not only that, so are Trevor and the kids. We're going to stay after Ciara's wedding and have our first European family vacation."

Maggie hugged Sarah. "I'm so happy, honey. You all deserve time away like this. How did you convince Trevor though? I thought he didn't want to take time off from work."

"Things are working out with his brothers. Both Wyatt and Clayton told him to go and that they'd cover for him. Devon is improving as well and Jacqui spends every day with him."

"I'm so glad to hear he's on the road to recovery. It was touch-and-go there for the first few days."

"Well, I'm off. You ladies enjoy the Great Captiva Bake-Off. See you tonight."

"Bye, Sarah," Jane said. "Don't let my unenthusiastic attitude worry you. I'm having a great time. Thanks for organizing everything."

"You're very welcome. Have fun."

Over the years, Diana had recorded every episode of Ina Garten's Barefoot Contessa, along with most of the Food Network's cooking shows.

Growing up, her family owned the largest house on the street. The ten-room home had three kitchens. The first floor kitchen was used for most of her family's meals. The second floor kitchen was in her grandparents' apartment, and the one in the basement was used by her grandfather.

He'd announce that he was going to the basement kitchen to watch over the roasting turkey or count the bottles of homemade wine in the wine cellar.

Everyone knew the real reason Grandpa went to the basement. It gave him the opportunity to smoke his cigars without the women nagging him to stop.

No matter her grandfather's use of the basement kitchen, Diana learned from her grandmother and mother how to make use of all the kitchens by baking the family's favorite desserts, some recipes having been passed down through three generations.

With her husband's encouragement, Diana finally opened her own bakery. Everyone in the family chipped in to help when she started out, but over the years she gained several loyal and hard-working employees to make the bakery a success.

Only recently she'd closed the bakery. It wasn't long after that she regretted her decision to retire. The months since closing she'd missed working more than she anticipated but didn't know what to do about it.

The plan to spend the day baking was not what Diana wanted to do but she couldn't say no. She wasn't certain whether today's activity was more for her benefit than the bride-to-be, but she could feel Jane's displeasure every time Maggie talked about baking. Diana couldn't help but feel responsible for ruining Jane's bachelorette party.

"Let first take a look at that cookbook of yours," Maggie said. "I'm dying to see what you've done so far."

The women gathered around the kitchen island. As Diana turned the pages of her book, the women made suggestions and comments encouraging her work.

"I can't believe how much you've already done. Diana, this book is ready to go. You don't need our help at all," Rachel said.

As they looked over the pages of Diana's cookbook, it was clear that the only thing keeping her from publishing the book was her lack of confidence.

"Why have you been dragging your heels on this all these months?" Chelsea asked.

Diana shrugged. "I don't know. I didn't think it was good enough to publish."

Kelly shook her head. "That's not the reason."

Everyone looked at Kelly.

"What do you mean?" Maggie asked.

"Diana, why did you retire? Was it your idea or your husband's?"

Maggie cringed. She didn't want Diana to feel cornered. "What does that have to do with anything?" Maggie asked.

Diana put her hand on Maggie's arm. "It's all right, Maggie. Kelly asks a good question. To be honest, I was feeling serious burnout. It's true that my husband suggested I seriously consider it, but in the end it was my call."

"But you regret it?" Chelsea asked.

Diana smiled. "Is it that obvious?"

Everyone laughed. "Um, yes, I would say so," Chelsea answered.

"Have I really been that bad?" Diana asked.

"Let's just say we've all been worried about you for a while now," Maggie answered. "I think you need to focus on publishing this book, and while you work on it, you'll find your passion again. I don't think you're ready to retire my dear."

Diana smiled. "I'll give it more thought. Thanks guys. I love you all so much. I don't know what I'd do without you. How about we get baking before I melt into a puddle of tears?"

"I've only got one question," Chelsea said. "Would we all do a better job at this baking thing if I made us a batch of Key Lime-tinis?"

Jane clapped her hands. "I thought you'd never ask."

Before the makeup and the sequined dresses, there was flour...and lots of it. The kitchen did indeed turn into a mess, but Riley and Iris insisted that everyone get cleaned up and ready for the sunset cruise.

Chelsea was the first to leave the inn, and when she arrived home, Grandma Sarah and Lauren were waiting.

"I'm so sorry about this, Chelsea. Descending on you at the last minute like this. We really appreciate you letting us stay here," Lauren said.

Hugging Lauren and then Grandma Sarah, Chelsea was dying to talk privately with Grandma Sarah.

"Not at all. I love having you here. I assume you both have settled in? Is there anything I can get you before I leave?"

Grandma Sarah shook her head. "I think we're fine. I hope you don't mind that we stopped at the market on the way here and put a few things in your refrigerator."

Chelsea looked at Grandma Sarah. "Oh good. At least you're familiar with the area and know where to get things. I'm so excited for you to finally be living down here with us. I hope you're as happy about the move as we are. I know it's difficult to leave your home after all these years."

"Yes, it was sad, but this is the next phase for me. Ever since I injured my ankle, I find that it's difficult to maneuver in the winter. So, where are you headed tonight?"

"We're all going on a sunset cruise with dinner and live music. Sarah arranged it for us."

"Sounds like fun," Lauren said.

"You know, the two of you should join us. I'm sure the ladies won't mind."

Grandma Sarah glared at Chelsea, and Chelsea knew immediately that she'd made an error.

"No, thank you, Chelsea. I think that Lauren and I should stay here tonight. It's been a long day as you can imagine. We got up at the crack of dawn."

"Of course. Well, I better get going. The girls are waiting and I don't want to be late for the limo. I believe we're getting the boat in Sanibel instead of Captiva, so we've got to drive a bit to get there. I might be late so I'll see you in the morning."

"Have fun," Lauren said.

Grandma Sarah had already turned her head, focusing on the television's local evening news.

Pulling up to the dock, Jane was the first out of the limo. The others followed and walked toward the three men in tuxedos.

The men escorted the women onto the boat and Jane beamed at being the first to catch their attention.

Sarah ignored her mother's suggestion that Jane was too old to wear a bride's sash, and so, the white and gold ribbon around Jane's body signified that she was VIP for the night.

As the boat sailed out on the Gulf waters, the waiters carried trays of champagne.

"This is so beautiful. I'd forgotten how gorgeous the sunsets are here," Rachel said. "We have some lovely sunsets on the Cape, but I think this one beats ours back home."

Jane raised her glass to her friends. "Thank you all for doing this for me. This is so amazing. I'm the luckiest woman to have you all for my best friends. Promise me that after I'm married, we will still get together like this as much as possible."

"Jane, you're not leaving the planet. You're just getting married," Chelsea said. "We haven't seen each other in months and it has nothing to do with any of our relationships. Maybe it's time you tell us what you're so worried about."

Everyone looked at Chelsea. Maggie was used to her best friend being so direct, but there was usually a lead up to such bluntness.

"Chelsea…" Maggie started.

Chelsea shook her head. "No, if we're really best friends, then we've got to talk about the elephant in the room…or in this case, on the boat."

No one said a word, and terror was the only way to describe Jane's look. She hesitated but then answered Chelsea. "I don't know. I'm fifty-four years old and I've never been married before. I don't know how I'm supposed to feel."

Maggie pointed to the corner where there was a leather sectional. "Let's all sit down over there and talk about this before they serve the food."

Everyone walked to the corner and Maggie asked the waiter to hold off on serving dinner until they were ready.

"Now, what's this all about?" Maggie asked.

Jane looked nervous but ready to talk. "Brian is a wonderful man. Yes, he has lots of money, but he is so much more than a billionaire. He's kind, his grown children and family are welcoming. As far as I can tell there isn't a flaw I can find."

Chelsea laughed. "Trust me, he has flaws. Look harder."

Maggie slapped Chelsea's hand. "Stop that."

"Of course, Chelsea's right. What I'm trying to say is that there isn't anything Brian has either done or said that's got me scared. I've been living my life on my terms for so long, I'm terrified of losing my autonomy."

"That's a good reason to be terrified," Rachel added. "But it doesn't mean that it's going to happen. Look at Maggie and me. We've been able to create the life we want and love and we're still able to trust again. Getting married shouldn't prevent you from being who you are. If it does, then maybe you shouldn't marry him."

Maggie looked at Rachel. "Are you seeing someone you haven't told us about?"

Rachel smiled. "We can talk about me later. This is about Jane."

Jane shook her head. "No, Brian hasn't indicated that he wants me to change in any way, but I'm nervous about it nonetheless."

"This problem is easily solved," Diana said. "Just talk to Brian and tell him how you feel. Depending on how he responds, you'll know what to do."

"Right, and if you don't, just get in touch with us on video and we'll add our two cents," Chelsea added.

Jane smiled. "Thanks guys. You're right. The first thing I'll do when I land back in Boston is go right to his office and talk this through."

Maggie shook her head. "I think you'd be better off to talk about this in a more private setting."

Jane laughed. "Oh, right. Good point."

"Do you guys think we can eat now? I'm starving," Kelly asked.

"Absolutely," Maggie said.

The women all raised their glasses once more, and Maggie added one last toast. "To Jane and Brian. May they enjoy many years of marital bliss and may our friendships last forever."

CHAPTER 23

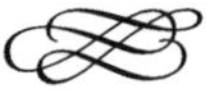

Michael called Maggie in the early morning hours the next day.

"Hey, Michael. How are you, honey?"

"I'm great, thanks. Brea and the kids are healthy and happy and the new puppy hasn't peed on the floor in almost a week. I call that progress, don't you?"

Maggie laughed at her son. Michael always found a way to make fun of any situation.

"I do indeed. Other than that, what's new in your world? How's it feel being back on the street instead of sitting behind a desk?"

"Oh, Mom, I can't tell you how happy I am to be back. At first, I was a little nervous, but it didn't take long to get back into the swing of things."

"I'm glad to hear it."

"Listen, the reason that I'm calling is I found out that Lauren flew down there with Grandma yesterday to help out with her move. I'm sure you noticed things are a little off with Lauren."

"What are you talking about? Lauren and your grandmother aren't here. My mother isn't due until Saturday."

"They're not? I'm positive Beth said that Lauren told her they were flying down yesterday. I guess Grandma didn't want to travel down by herself and asked Lauren to go with her."

"I'm sure Beth got the day wrong. If they were here, I'd know about it, but it's good to know that Lauren is coming down. I'd like to see her."

"Oh, okay. Well, in any case, before you see her, I wanted to let you know that my therapist is willing to see Lauren if she wants to talk to someone. Chris and I were talking the other day that we think she'd benefit from some professional help. It worked wonders for both Chris and me."

"Thank you, honey. That's a very good suggestion and I'm sure when Lauren is ready, she'll get in touch with your therapist. I've now talked to several of you who think she needs help. I need to see her myself. I'll know if Lauren is in trouble."

"Of course, but..."

"Michael, honey, I've got to go. I've got so much to do today. How about I call you after I've seen Lauren? Maybe Sunday?"

"Sure, Mom. I'll talk to you then. Love you."

"Love you, too, sweetie. Say hello to Brea and the kids from Grandma."

"Will do."

Maggie rushed off the phone with Michael because she knew Beth didn't get her days mixed up. She was about to ring her mother when Chelsea walked into the kitchen.

"Good morning, sunshine," Chelsea said. "Wasn't last night wonderful? Those waiters weren't hard on the eyes either."

Sitting on a stool at the kitchen island, Maggie tapped her nails on the quartz counter.

"I'm glad you're here, Chelsea. I'm about to call my mother and you can keep me from losing my cool."

"Losing your cool? About what?"

"Michael just called me. Apparently, my mother and Lauren flew down here yesterday and didn't tell me. Now, I have no idea what's going on with Lauren, but for my mother not to get in touch with me when she knows perfectly well that I'm beside myself over Lauren…well, that's so inconsiderate. I'm calling her right now."

Chelsea finished filling her coffee cup, put it down and took Maggie's cellphone from her.

"You don't need to call your mother."

"What?"

"They're staying at my place," Chelsea explained. "They should be here in about fifteen minutes. Lauren just got out of the shower when I walked over here."

"They're staying with you? Why didn't you tell me?"

"Your mother asked me not to. I figured it wasn't such a big deal since you'd see them today. What's one little day?"

"It's bad enough that they kept this from me, but you? You're my best friend. I don't care what my mother told you to do, you're supposed to be on my team," Maggie fumed.

"I am on your team, but…well, your mother scares me."

Maggie rolled her eyes. "Nothing scares you, Chelsea Marsden.

Chelsea nodded. "Yes, you're right, nothing except your mother.

Just then, Lauren and Grandma Sarah walked into the kitchen.

"Don't be mad at Chelsea, Maggie. She was nice enough to let us stay at her place. I got my days mixed up and got here a little early. I knew you had company so I called Chelsea. What's the big deal?"

Maggie sighed. "No big deal I guess. I just worry about you, that's all."

"Grandma was in good hands, Mom," Lauren added.

Maggie hugged Lauren. "Hello, sweetheart. I'm glad to see you." She then hugged her mother, "You too, Mom."

"Oh, scones. Mom, you made scones. Can I have one?"

"Of course you can. Help yourself."

"Where is everyone?" Grandma Sarah asked.

"Still sleeping," Maggie said. "I'm sure they'll be down soon. So, what's the plan? When do the movers arrive?"

"Saturday afternoon. I'm going to have to watch them closely. I've heard scary stories about movers breaking things."

Matteo was up and in the dining room before anyone else.

"Who's that?" Grandma Sarah asked.

"He's a guest. He's our only guest."

"You mean he's here while your friends are visiting?"

"Mr. Benedetti will be with us for a while longer. So, what are you two doing today? You're welcome to join us if you'd like. I have to check with Sarah, but I think we've got a free day of doing whatever we want."

"I wouldn't mind spending the day relaxing on the beach," Lauren offered. "Grandma, what do you want to do?"

"Right now, I think I'd like some breakfast. Maggie, dear, do you mind if I eat in the dining room?"

"Of course not. Just tell Riley what you want and she'll bring it out to you."

Grandma looked at Riley. "I'll start with some coffee please. Lauren, what about you?"

"I'm good with a scone and coffee."

One by one, the lunch-bunch ladies joined them in the kitchen."

Jane still had her pajamas and bathrobe on. "Can someone hook me up to an IV of coffee? I'm not awake yet."

Riley laughed as she poured Jane a cup. "I've got you covered, here you go."

"Bless you," Jane said.

"Don't look now, but Mr. Benedetti has been cornered by your mother," Chelsea whispered.

"Oh no!" Maggie said. "I forgot he was in there. What should we do?"

Lauren peeked around the corner. "I think you should leave them alone. By the look on your guest's smiling face, he's not too unhappy about having breakfast with Grandma," Lauren answered.

"Mind if I join you?" Grandma asked Matteo.

He looked up and smiled. "Not at all. Have a seat. Please excuse me for not getting up."

"What's wrong with your leg?" Grandma Sarah asked.

"My leg was severely injured in a car accident many years ago. Combined with a hip surgery on the same side, it makes stability a problem sometimes."

Grandma shrugged. "Is that all? You're lucky, most of my friends are either on tons of medications or dead. You look a little peaked though, are you all right?"

"Some days the pain is worse than others, but I manage. How is it that you are visiting the inn? I thought I was the only guest, except for Mrs. Moretti's friends."

Grandma Sarah nodded. "You are the only guest…well, paying guest that is. I'm Maggie's mother, Sarah Garrison."

Grandma reached across the table and offered her hand. "And you are?"

"Matteo Benedetti," he answered as he shook Grandma Sarah's hand.

Riley brought out Grandma Sarah's breakfast of scrambled eggs, hash brown potatoes, toast and a side of cut-up fruit.

"Thank you, Riley. This looks delicious."

"So, where are you from, Mr. Benedetti?"

"Matteo, please. I live in Bonita Springs. Only about a forty-five minute drive from here."

Her brow furrowed. "I don't understand. If you live so close, why are you here? I mean, why spend the money?"

He laughed at her question. "I guess that does seem a bit strange, doesn't it? Let's just say I needed to get away from home."

"The wife bugging you, huh?"

He shook his head. "No, my wife passed away eighteen months ago. It's just me and my brother, Ralph. His legal name is Raffaele, but we call him Ralph."

"I'm sorry about your wife. I lost my husband about ten years ago…heart attack."

"Oh how awful. I don't know what's worse, watching someone fade away from an illness like cancer, or a sudden loss."

"Both are horrible if you ask me," she answered.

Matteo nodded. "I believe you're right."

"Do you ever get lonely?" Grandma Sarah asked.

He nodded. "I do, but my brother and his wife are nearby, so that helps. Having family close is a good thing."

"That's how I feel too. That's why I've come down to Florida. I'm moving into a new condo in a few days."

"How wonderful. Where are you from?"

"Massachusetts. I've lived there for most of my life…certainly, my married life. I was born in Scotland. Do you mind me asking you how old you are?"

If Matteo was annoyed by Grandma Sarah's direct questions, he didn't let on. "I'm seventy-six, why do you ask?"

"Just wondering. I'm pushing eighty myself, and I don't like it one bit. I plan to have as much fun as I can though. Now that I don't have to contend with the snow and winters, I should be partying all year long."

"Sounds like a marvelous idea," he said.

"Maybe I'll get your cellphone number and we can get together now and then. I'm not interested in a romance, just looking to meet new friends."

Matteo leaned closer to her. "I'm very happy to have made your acquaintance, Sarah Garrison."

They ate their breakfast and when Matteo was finished, he got up from his chair and shook Grandma Sarah's hand.

"I hope you love Florida as much as I do. The weather is fantastic, and the people are very nice."

"Thank you. I know I will."

Leaning on his cane, she watched him walk away from the dining room and out the front door. He didn't offer up his phone or any other method of contact, and Grandma Sarah didn't push the request further.

What she could tell, however, was that Matteo Benedetti was hiding something. Whatever it was, she figured the man was entitled to his privacy.

Grandma Sarah carried her empty plate back to the kitchen.

"What was that all about?" Maggie asked.

"You mean, Mr. Benedetti? Oh, we just talked and enjoyed a nice breakfast. Thank you, Riley."

"You're very welcome, Mrs. Garrison."

"He seems very nice. Too bad about his wife though. It's a tough thing the first couple of years."

Maggie pressed her mother for more information. "What exactly did he say? Did he tell you much about his life?"

"Maggie, dear, why are you so interested in Mr. Benedetti? Leave the man alone. We all have secrets…or at least things we don't want to share with others."

"So, you agree that he's hiding something?"

Grandma Sarah nodded. "Most definitely."

Frustrated, Maggie decided to focus on her friends and not worry about Mr. Benedetti. However, since they weren't going far today, perhaps she'd take another shot at talking to him. Before the day was over, Maggie hoped to learn more about her mysterious guest.

CHAPTER 24

Sarah arrived at the inn just in time to join everyone for breakfast.

"What in the world are you two doing here?" She asked while hugging her grandmother and then Lauren.

"Your grandmother got the dates wrong on the move. Fortunately, she didn't give the movers the wrong date when she booked them weeks ago," Maggie explained.

Everyone was talking at the same time as Maggie walked out the back door and looked over at Matteo who was sitting under the gazebo.

"I'll be right back," she announced. "You all catch up with each other."

Walking toward Matteo, she waved. "Good morning, Matteo. How are you doing today?"

"I'm feeling a little stronger I think. It's another beautiful day, so I thought I'd sit here for a spell before it got too hot."

"I take it that you're not one for the beach?"

"I wouldn't say that. I love the water, it's just that my leg won't cooperate. My wife and I used to go to the beach all the time."

"I'm sorry about earlier. I hope my mother didn't bother you at breakfast. She sometimes can seem..."

"Direct?" he asked.

Maggie laughed. "Yes, that's a nice way to put it."

"Your mother is charming, Maggie. Now I understand better where you grew up. You lived in Massachusetts, how did you end up here on Captiva, and how did you meet your husband?"

"Oh, it's a long story. I don't want to trouble you with all that."

"It's no trouble. I want to know," he insisted.

"Well, I was married before and we had five children. They're all grown up with families of their own now. My husband and I... well, we were married over thirty years but it wasn't always a good marriage." She then shrugged. "Whatever a good marriage is..."

"Oh, good marriages leave clues. I'm sure you and your husband had some good years. That's a long time to be married."

She nodded. "Yes, that's true. But he wasn't always...um..." Maggie searched for the right word.

"Faithful?" he said.

"My goodness, I guess my discomfort with talking about Daniel comes through loud and clear, doesn't it? Anyway, yes, you're right. Just before we were to divorce, he had a heart attack and died. He had asked me for a divorce only two days before he died. He said that he was in love with someone else. Can you imagine that?"

She waited for Matteo to squirm in his chair at the awkwardness of her story, but he stayed focused on her and didn't seem upset by anything she'd said.

"How long after his death did you remarry?"

"Two years. I came to Captiva to get away from everything I was dealing with. I met Paolo here, as well as the woman who owned this property before us."

"A tropical love story," he said.

"I don't think I'd describe it that way. Paolo and I were left this property when the woman died. It wasn't an inn at that time. It was her residence, but had, years earlier, been an active and very popular vacation property. They called it the Key Lime Garden Inn, so we kept that name. Paolo and I resurrected it and brought life and a bit of romance back into the place."

"And into your heart," he said.

Maggie blushed. "Yes. I suppose so."

"My, you are brave," he said.

Maggie didn't know what to make of that statement.

"I'm not so sure about that," she answered him.

"You were left with an unresolved situation that was completely out of your control, and you didn't let it stop you from building a new life with someone. I'd call that very brave. It takes a lot to trust someone with your heart once again. Paolo must be very special. You certainly are."

Since Daniel's death, there had been countless moments like this one where Maggie had to revisit a time that had caused her so much pain. In those moments she had to make a choice to wallow in the pain and suffer once more or push it to the far reaches of her brain and put one foot in front of the other, moving forward.

"Thank you for saying that. It's a choice. I've made it over and over in my mind several times," she explained.

Matteo nodded. "That's what we have to do, isn't it? Every day we make a choice to keep living or start dying. The funny thing is that there are so many ways to die. I didn't always know that, but I've found that the worst death is the one where you're still alive but everything around you has ceased to exist."

Maggie was stunned. What Matteo described was exactly how she felt after Daniel died but was unable to explain to anyone. Now, sitting in front of Matteo, a relative stranger, she understood that her situation wasn't unique at all.

She felt a deep sadness in this truth. To think there were so many suffering in private made her already empathetic heart much more sensitive. She could see that at this moment, Matteo was talking about himself.

"What are you choosing, Matteo?"

He looked at her and smiled. "Today, I choose to enjoy this beautiful weather, to feel the sun on my face, and to share a few moments first with your mother, and now with you."

After several minutes, Maggie left Matteo to rejoin her friends but she couldn't stop thinking about what he'd said to her.

She'd come out to the gazebo to get more information about Matteo and walked away knowing little about the man except that he was very sick and ready to leave the Key Lime Garden Inn and the world just as soon as he was called.

Wyatt reached for the doorknob twice but didn't turn it. He'd paced the hall in front of his father's library for the last hour, during which time a nurse, the maid, and a doctor went inside.

He'd thought more than once about leaving and trying this at a better time, but then realized that there was no better time and there never would be. It was only after everyone had left and his father was alone that Wyatt finally went into the library.

His father looked better than the last time Wyatt visited him in the hospital, but still frail and helpless.

Devon looked up at him and smiled. It wasn't a full smile, at least the result wasn't, but Wyatt could tell that his father was very happy to see him.

"Hey, Dad."

"My…son." Devon's arm was no longer paralyzed and so he reached up to touch Wyatt. Wyatt bent down and put his arms around his father as best he could.

"You look good. How are you feeling?"

"Better…where…have you…been?"

"I'm sorry I haven't come to see you sooner. I've been pretty busy. You know how it is."

Devon nodded. "Sit…stay."

Wyatt sat across from his father and the awkward silence between them made him want to run out of the room, but he didn't leave. He stayed, just as Trevor asked, and as his father now demanded. He thought it appropriate that even in the wheelchair, Devon Hutchins took control of the room.

"Are you…happy?"

Wyatt didn't expect his father to care one way or the other. If his father wasn't so ill, he might have said so, but now all he could do was nod. "I'm ok, at least for now."

"I want…I want you to stay."

Devon looked at Wyatt and wouldn't turn away until Wyatt answered him. He figured to keep the peace there was no harm in agreeing.

"I'm not going anywhere, Dad."

Wyatt didn't notice Jacqui standing in the doorway.

"Can I see you for a minute?" she asked her brother.

"Dad, I'll be right back. I've got to talk to Jacqui."

Wyatt followed Jacqui out into the foyer.

"What are you doing?" she asked.

"I'm sorry? What specifically are you talking about?"

Jacqui walked to the library door and closed it so Devon wouldn't hear them talking. "Specifically, I mean, why are you lying to Dad? You and I both know that when you feel the time is right to bolt, you're out of here. Why get his hopes up?"

Wyatt leaned against the foyer table and crossed his arms. "Sweet, little Jacqui. I hear that ever since Dad's stroke, you've been by his side taking care of him. What's with the Florence Nightingale bit? You and Dad were never close as I remember it. Is it guilt or do you have an angle I haven't figured out yet?"

"Everyone has to have an angle with you. Isn't it possible that I love my father and don't want him to die?"

Wyatt put his finger to his cheek, tapping it in a supposed moment of introspection. "Um, no. That's not it. Try again."

Jacqui moved closer to him and pointed her finger in his chest. "He's making progress and soon, he'll be back in the office and you'll be out on your..."

"Wyatt, I didn't know you were here," their mother Eliza said as she walked to the front door. She stopped and air-kissed Wyatt and then Jacqui. "I'm heading out to get my nails done. Are the two of you staying with your father? The occupational nurse is supposed to be here soon. It would be great if either one or both of you could stay until she gets here. I'd do it but my nails are a disaster."

Jacqui nodded. "Sure, Mom. I'll stay."

Jacqui looked at Wyatt and smiled. "Wyatt was just leaving."

"That's great. Well, I'm off," Eliza said.

When they were alone again, Jacqui stared at Wyatt defiantly.

"Tell Dad I'll come back another day to see him...or don't, but I'll be back."

Wyatt knew this first meeting would be difficult, but he hadn't counted on Jacqui hovering. The process of gaining his father's affections was threatened by his sister's constant interference.

As he walked to his car, he decided at the very least he'd need to stick around to see what his little sister was up to. When he figured that out, he'd be sure to broadcast her plans to the family.

Process of elimination...check!

Sarah, Lauren and Grandma Sarah joined the lunch-bunch ladies on the beach. Although Sarah and Maggie's mother were having a good time, Lauren seemed distracted and couldn't sit still for more than five minutes at a time.

"So Rachel, how are things at the Vineyard? We never did get to the Cape last summer," Maggie asked.

"I know, and believe me, you were missed. I love my job but it's a far cry from the world of teaching fifth-graders."

"I can imagine. You must have dirty hands and clothes all the time," Jane said.

Rachel nodded. "Not all the time, but often. Everyone thinks that when you run a vineyard, you're in the field all day, every day, but there are a million other things to do that don't involve getting your hands in dirt."

Maggie watched Lauren walk back and forth to and from the water, cellphone plastered to her ear. She looked to be deep in a serious discussion and could only assume it was her husband Jeff on the other end of the line.

When she returned to her chair, she looked upset.

"Was that Jeff?" Maggie asked.

Lauren nodded.

"Is everything okay?"

Lauren waved her mother off with a hand. It was obvious to Maggie and anyone else who heard them, that her daughter didn't want to talk about it. Whatever was wrong, like everything else happening with Lauren these days, no one was privy to her thoughts.

Worry hit Maggie like a hammer, and when she looked over at Chelsea, her mother, and then Sarah, she could tell that she wasn't the only one concerned about Lauren's state of mind.

She thought about Michael's call. Maybe he and Christopher were right about Lauren needing to see a psychiatrist. She desperately wanted to help her daughter, but Maggie had no idea how to approach her or what to say.

More than anything, Maggie finally could see that her daughter wasn't the same, and it terrified her. Lauren was headed into the sixth month of her pregnancy. Maggie knew nothing about depression, but she was concerned that the baby might feel Lauren's anxieties.

Kelly's question startled Maggie.

"I think it's a great idea. What do you think, Maggie?"

"I'm sorry, what are we talking about?"

"Jane wants to rent Jet Skis. Are you in?"

"Not this time. I'm happy just soaking up the sun. You all go ahead though. Just walk to the left and a bit in front of The Mucky Duck and you'll see them. Look for Powell Water Sports. Joshua and Luke Powell will be there to rent them. Tell them that you're friends of mine and maybe you can get a discount."

Jane, Diana, Kelly and Rachel ventured off to rent Jet Skis, while Maggie, Chelsea, Sarah, Lauren and Grandma Sarah stayed behind.

Lauren jumped out of her chair. "I'm going for a walk."

"Okay, honey. Do you want someone to go with you?"

Lauren walked away. "I won't be long."

After she left, Grandma Sarah looked at Maggie and shook her finger. "You've got to talk to her. She needs her mother."

"What do I say? She's not breaking down crying and there is no indication that she wants my help."

"Mom, that alone should tell you how bad this is," Sarah added. "If she won't talk to you, then something is really wrong."

Maggie's heart broke for her daughter. She'd talk to Paolo about it after dinner. Maybe he had some idea what to do. She looked off at the horizon and prayed for a miracle and for the wisdom to help her daughter find her way.

CHAPTER 25

Manicures, pedicures, a facial, and a massage were all Jane could talk about. "I'm so ready to be pampered while drinking a mimosa. What about you ladies?"

"Look at the glum faces. I can't believe it, but none of us cares about a spa day," Chelsea whispered to Maggie. "This is the most depressing and insipid bachelorette party week I think I've ever had."

Maggie made a face. "Really, Chelsea? Exactly how many of these things have you actually attended?"

Chelsea thought for a minute. "You know, you're right, this is my first...and last."

"Oh stop. This was all designed for Jane and she's having a blast. Look at her. Her feet have hardly touched the ground since she got up this morning. Not to mention, my daughter went to a lot of trouble setting all these activities in place. We have to have fun for her sake, if not Jane's."

"Well, I guess that's something," Chelsea remarked. "I'm just tired of having to remind Jane that we're all in our mid- to late-fifties, except Rachel, and not in our twenties. She's acting like she just graduated college and we're her sorority sisters ready to party like it's 1985."

"Think of it this way. Did you go to your prom?" Maggie asked.

"No, I did not. Why?"

"Well Jane might be middle-aged but she's experiencing something that usually young women experience. Aren't you still a little sad that you never went to your prom?"

Chelsea shook her head. "No."

"Not even a little?"

"Nope."

"What is wrong with you? Don't you have a nostalgic bone in your body?"

"Of course I do. I miss a lot of things from when I was younger. I don't miss my 1985 hairdo, but other than that, there are tons of things I miss."

"Like what?"

"My hair. I had more hair. I was thinner and I miss my Walkman, oh, and my Ford Escort."

Maggie shook her head. "No. No one misses their Ford Escort."

"Yes, I do."

"Anyway, are you getting my point? Jane is doing what we all did when we were in our twenties. For her, this is her twenties."

Clipboard in hand, Sarah walked into the kitchen. "Is everyone ready to go?"

"Sarah, honey, you need to chill. Next thing you'll be wearing a headset and talking into a megaphone. It's just a bunch of women going to the spa. We're not marching to go to war," Chelsea said.

Maggie giggled and kissed Sarah's cheek. "Good job, sweetie. We'll see you later. Don't you have packing to do or something?"

Maggie couldn't stop laughing as they made their way to the van.

Diana pulled Maggie aside and whispered, "Maggie, I was wondering if you'd mind my staying here for one or two more days after the girls leave. I need a little time alone and I just don't think I'll be ready to leave when they do."

"Of course you can stay. We don't leave for Italy for another five days. We might be running around getting ready."

"Oh, that's all right. I don't need anyone to do anything for me. I'm just looking for a bit of solitude. Maybe some alone time on the beach. I remember you talking about your early morning walks collecting seashells. That sounds like heaven to me."

"I tell you what. How about when we get back tonight I will show you a few books that helped me when I first found this place. Come see me in the library before dinner. I have something special I think you'll like."

"Thanks, Maggie. I really appreciate this."

Maggie smiled and knew exactly what Diana was looking for, and she couldn't wait to show her *A Gift from the Sea* and the journals of Rose Johnson Lane.

Devon watched his daughter as they played Checkers. Jacqui could feel his gaze and she wondered what he was thinking but not saying.

"Dad, I might regret this, but can you tell me what you're thinking?"

"Where are you…going?"

"Where am I going? I'm not going anywhere. I'm staying right here with you."

"No!" he declared emphatically.

Jacqui recognized his frustration at not being able to get the words out, but she didn't know how to help him.

"I don't understand," she explained.

He tried again. "What will…you…be?"

She finally understood what he wanted.

"You want to know what my plans are now that I've graduated?"

His eyes lit up. "Yes."

She smiled. "You and me both, Dad. I'm trying to figure that out. Right now, I'm leaning on staying in New York. After all, that's probably the best place for an artist like me to live. I'd come back home to Florida if I had a job using my talent as an artist. I've talked to Chelsea about it but I haven't come up with any answers just yet."

Devon pointed his finger down to the table and tapped it. "Here."

Jacqui understood everything now. Her father wanted her to stay in Florida. It was her first choice as well, but she didn't know what she would do for a living if she did and she didn't want to be supported by her father. Those days were over for her. She'd become a responsible adult and was proud of her achievements since leaving home.

"Dad, I promise you. If I can find a job here, I'll stay. I'm not in a hurry to leave. I want to stay for the summer and figure things out. How does that sound?"

Devon smiled and nodded his head. "Good."

"What's he doing?" Diana asked Maggie.

"Mr. Benedetti?"

Sitting on the back porch swing, they watched as Matteo turned the pages of a large book. He was sitting on the ground in the middle of the vegetable garden.

When Paolo came onto the porch, Maggie asked him why their guest was on the ground.

"Did he fall? Does he need help?" Maggie asked.

Paolo shook his head. "He asked me to come back in an hour

and help him up. I asked him if he wanted to come inside now instead of in an hour."

"What did he say?"

"He said if he did that he wouldn't be able to smell the dirt."

"Smell the dirt? What in the world?" Maggie asked "You should have told him that we could put a pile of the garden dirt in a bowl for him. He could keep it in his room."

"That is the most bizarre thing I think I've ever seen," Riley said, watching from the back door. "Do you think he's a gardener?"

"He's not engaging with the soil at all. He's looking through a photo album," Paolo said.

Maggie shook her head, "He couldn't have done that in his bedroom?"

Paolo shrugged. "Maggie I have no idea what he's doing, I just work here."

Maggie laughed and kissed her husband on the cheek. "And a good employee you are too."

Maggie and Diana went inside and filled their glasses with more iced tea.

"I'm so glad we didn't go down to the beach when we got home from the spa," Diana said. "Between the sun that I got the other day and the exfoliating scrub my skin got at the spa, I'm in pain."

"Me too," Maggie said. "Let's get to my office before the girls come back. It's pizza night and if my stomach is any barometer, our friends are getting hungry too."

They walked into Maggie's office and Diana took a deep breath. "Lilacs?"

Maggie smiled. "Well, for now, it's only a candle. We'd have to fly home to Massachusetts in late April to get the real thing. Lilacs are my favorite but they don't grow much down here. We have too many hot months here. Have a seat."

Diana watched the butterflies swarming around the bush just outside Maggie's window.

"My dear friend Rose used this room as her office and bedroom. She would sit in this chair and write in her journal for hours."

"And now that's what you do?" Diana asked.

"As often as I can. My family's issues and running the inn keeps me pretty busy most days. Whenever I can, I sneak in here and do a little writing. I've been collecting women's fiction books for a while now. I love how many of them deal with a woman's need to find her place in the world. Rose shared several books from her collection and I've kept them here in this room. You're welcome to sit here for as long as you'd like. Perhaps you'll find something that speaks to you."

"Thank you, Maggie. I guess it's no secret that I'm at loose ends these days. It's not just the retirement from the bakery. It feels deeper than that. You must have felt that way after Daniel…I mean when you decided to move here. You changed your life and look at you now. I envy you."

Maggie sat and looked out the window before speaking.

"I do love it here. Captiva has been my refuge, the home that I made for myself when I felt lost and untethered from everything I believed in. But…just when I started to feel that I had control over my life, I got cancer. Nothing throws your world upside-down like a cancer diagnosis."

"But you beat it. You're cancer-free, right?"

Maggie nodded. "I am…or, as they say, there is no evidence of cancer in my body. But I go back in October for more scans because that's how cancer works. It keeps you feeling like a patient for years, even after they can't find any."

"Are you nervous?" Diana asked.

"I'm always nervous every time it's scan day. But, another thing cancer does is it makes you appreciate every day that you're alive so much more. When I look at Paolo, or my family, I'm so much more in love with them than I was before the disease. Colors are more vibrant and the world looks more beautiful. Captiva sunsets before and during chemo were nothing compared to the ones I saw when my treatment was over."

"I can't imagine what you've gone through. I don't think I could do that. I'm not as strong as you, Maggie."

Maggie took Diana's hand in hers. "Dear Diana, my point is that it's okay to recognize those loose end days, but then, as soon as you can, put them in a box and store them away. After you've done that, get back to living and loving your life as quickly as possible. You only have one you know."

"I want pizza," Jane yelled from the kitchen.

Maggie and Diana laughed. "They're back. I guess we better get out there and feed everyone. Come in here as often as you need. This is the best room in the house."

"Thanks, Maggie. Don't forget to have Paolo pick Mr. Benedetti off the ground."

CHAPTER 26

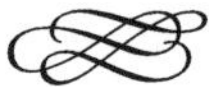

Despite the early hour, Lauren left Chelsea's house carrying a small bucket and started for the beach. She was surprised to find so many people already gathering and looking for the perfect spot to spend the day. Even though the sun hadn't risen in the sky, it was already hot.

Lauren removed her sandals and walked to the edge of the water. Her head down, she searched for the seashells that would make the journey from sand to bucket and eventually Chelsea's house.

When her mother moved to Captiva a few years earlier, she talked of her early morning walks along this very beach and how she'd come to find herself through hours watching the water, reading about Captiva and writing in her journals.

Lauren could understand how her mother fell in love with the island and her new life, and Lauren felt jealous that she didn't have the same landscape back home.

Nonetheless, she accepted that it was her own fault. She hadn't carved out quiet moments for herself, instead afraid of what those moments might evoke.

She told herself that it was better to be busy. Her children needed her, and Jeff depended on Lauren's capable and independent ways.

The business was thriving and she took pride in knowing that it was hard work and many hours that built it into the successful real estate agency that it was. She was a strong and determined woman, and that was more important than anything else.

It was harder to say goodbye to her friends than Maggie thought. They'd celebrate Jane's engagement and fall back into patterns of joking and teasing along with serious conversations as if no time at all had passed.

With promises to keep up with their monthly video get-togethers, Jane reminded the women that they must save the date on their calendars for her wedding.

"It's good that Diana is staying for a couple more days," Rachel whispered. "She needs time to think about what happens next for her. Thank you, Maggie, for letting us celebrate here. It was so special. Let's work on getting everyone to the Cape next summer."

"I think that would be wonderful, Rachel. Thank you."

Jane threw her arms around Maggie. "Thank you dear friend. We all had so much fun. Thank Sarah for me, will you?"

"I will," Maggie said.

Kelly hugged Chelsea and then Maggie. "You guys are the best. I'm so glad you have each other. Captiva is lucky to have the two of you to keep things hopping. Now that your mother is living here, I can't wait to hear all kinds of stories about the trouble you three will get into."

Diana, Maggie and Chelsea waved to the women as their van drove down the driveway and out onto the street.

"I wish Lauren had come to say goodbye. Is she still at your place?" Maggie asked.

Chelsea nodded. "Last I saw, your mother was on my computer shopping for a car."

"On the computer?" Maggie asked.

"Yes, that's how the young people buy cars now, at least that's how your mother explained it to me."

Maggie sighed. "And so it begins."

The aroma of bacon and eggs wafted through the kitchen.

"Paolo said he had a craving for bacon and eggs," Riley said.

"There goes his cholesterol," Maggie said.

"Everyone gone?" Riley asked.

"Yup. I already miss them."

"Me too," Diana added.

Just then, Millie walked into the kitchen. "I'm back and reporting for duty," she announced. "How did the reunion go?"

"Well, I think. Everyone seemed to have a good time," Maggie answered.

"I've got my work cut out for me today. I'd better get to it. But first, did I mention that I haven't had breakfast? I could smell the bacon all the way to the driveway."

Maggie laughed. "Fine. Have something to eat before you start work. How was your time off? Did you do anything fun?"

"I spent some time with my sister's family. It was good to see them again. We're still getting to know each other after all these years."

"Oh, I'm sorry, Diana, this is Millie Brenner. She's our new housekeeper and bookkeeper. Millie, this is my friend, Diana. She's staying a couple extra days."

"Nice to meet you, Diana. I understand not wanting to go back home. Captiva is hard to leave."

"You've got that right. As a matter of fact, I'm going to take a walk on the beach right now. I'll catch up with you all later. Nice to meet you, Millie."

"I'll get to cleaning the bedrooms right after breakfast," Millie said.

"I should mention that Mr. Benedetti is still with us. I'm not exactly sure for how much longer, but we're all leaving for Italy in a few days so if he stays after we've gone, you, Riley and Iris will need to take care of him and make sure he has everything he needs."

"Of course. Not to worry. We all can handle it."

"Also, my mother has moved down to Florida and my daughter Lauren came down with her to help her move into her condo. They're staying at Chelsea's house for now, but you might see them here and there walking around the property."

Millie nodded, taking in everything Maggie said.

Maggie shook her head. "I'm sorry that I seem so frantic, but I'm juggling several balls in the air. I'm headed to the carriage house to start packing for our trip before the day comes and I'm not ready. Thank heaven our passports are up-to-date."

"Don't worry about a thing, Maggie. You go do what you have to do. We can handle the house."

"Oh, one more thing. You might have noticed the pile of lumber in the driveway. Paolo has been working on building something at the back of the property. It will have to be put on hold while we're away. Please make sure no one disturbs that area."

Millie nodded. "Got it."

"Well, that's everything I can think of right now. I'll catch up with you later if I think of anything more."

Maggie poured a glass of iced tea and headed for the carriage house and a day of packing and planning for their trip to Italy. She looked forward to visiting Italy once more, but her lingering worries about Lauren meant that she'd be leaving the country and away from her daughter.

As much as it hurt Maggie, she had to admit that it didn't seem to matter how far away she was. Lauren didn't notice her even when she stood right in front of her.

Maggie blamed herself for not doing more for her daughter. She pushed that thought away and told herself that attitude wouldn't help anyone, least of all Lauren.

Her bucket full, Lauren made her way to the path leading to the Key Lime Garden Inn. She remembered her mother telling her about the day she found the path and her new friend, the property owner, Rose Johnson Lane. Imagining her mother's experience, the view looked different for Lauren than it did for Maggie.

Lauren walked the path and navigated around all the lumber in place for Paolo's latest project. The inn had gone through so many updates and so much construction since her mother's first visit to the property.

A koi pond, several bird feeders and two birdbaths as well as a new shed and many new additions to the flower garden, made the back of the property Lauren's favorite spot.

Looking near the koi pond she saw Mr. Benedetti leaning against a tree, his cane by his side and a photo album on the ground. His eyes were closed and he looked so peaceful she didn't want to disturb him. Quietly walking on tiptoes as she passed, she cringed when she stepped on a twig and cracked it.

"You're Lauren, isn't that right?" he asked.

Lauren smiled. "Yes, and I'm so sorry I woke you."

"I wasn't sleeping," he said. "What's in the bucket?"

"A few seashells," she answered.

"May I see them?" he asked.

Lauren nodded and sat on the bench next to him. She thought

it odd that rather than sit on the bench, he chose the ground and the tree.

"You must have been up early this morning to get this many seashells."

"I was. I got up just after sunrise. What about you? Were you up early as well?" she asked.

"Yes. I've been waiting for you," he said.

Unnerved by his comment, Lauren felt she should leave and get back to Chelsea's house. "I'm sorry, I don't understand what you mean."

"I'd like to tell you a story if you're not in a hurry to get back home."

Lauren nodded. She felt uneasy but there was something about him that kept her frozen in place. If not for her mother's opinion of her guest, she would have been gone already.

"Can you help me up and onto the bench?" he asked.

"Oh, of course."

Lauren bent down and put her arms under his as he leaned on his cane. At first, she wasn't sure she'd be able to lift him on her own, but with the cane's assistance she was able to get him settled on the bench.

"Hand me that photo album if you would."

She placed the book on his lap and he rested his cane against the bench beside him. He handed the photo album to Lauren. "Take a look. These are the photos of my life."

As she turned the pages she saw pictures of a much younger man. "Is this you?"

He nodded and pointed to the two other people in the photos. "That's my wife and my daughter."

"They're beautiful. You have a beautiful family."

"We were very close, the three of us. We traveled all over the world together. I've carried this photo album with me along my journey to revisit these places once more."

Lauren noticed the last few pictures were of Captiva.

"So, you've been to Captiva before...with your family?"

He closed the photo album, put it beside him and then turned to look at Lauren.

"Where is your family, Lauren?"

Her hand went to her stomach and her baby. It was a protective and immediate reaction. Her heart raced as she realized that she'd never told him her name, nor had she spent any time with him before.

Assuming her mother or grandmother told him, she answered, "My husband and two daughters are at home in Massachusetts.

"And, you have another on the way soon."

"Yes."

He got up from the bench and reached for his cane. "Would you help me, Lauren? I'd like to walk out onto the street and I can't do it myself."

Lauren steadied him and reached for the photo album.

"Leave it. I'll get it later," he said.

As they walked out to the front and down the driveway, Lauren silently questioned the wisdom of continuing as he seemed weaker by the minute.

Once away from the property, they walked to the intersection of Andy Rosse Lane and the main road.

"There is a bench across the street in front of the Royal Shell real estate agency. We can sit there."

Glad that she'd remembered her cellphone, Lauren worried if he was strong enough to walk back to the inn. She decided that if she had to, she'd call her mother and get someone to help them.

They sat in silence for a few minutes before he spoke.

He lifted his cane and pointed. "My wife was across the street and Gia and I were over here. This real estate place wasn't here but some of these buildings were. Of course, The Bubble Room was here. Gia loved The Bubble Room."

Lauren smiled. "I love that place too."

"I was holding Gia's hand. I told her to wait for her mother to cross the street but she let go and started to run. I ran after her but we couldn't avoid the car. He was going so fast. There wasn't anything I could do.'

He turned to look at Lauren. With tears in his eyes he repeated his words, "She let go of my hand."

Terror hit Lauren in her stomach as she realized what he was saying. She put her arm through his and kept him close.

"I was in the hospital for several weeks. My leg was crushed in so many places, they thought they'd have to amputate. My wife wasn't hurt…but Gia…my Gia…she was gone."

He pulled a cloth from his pocket and wiped his eyes.

"After the accident, my wife was never the same. I don't think either of us were. We stopped traveling, she…my wife…she seemed to give up living. Gia was dead and my wife…well, she was dead too. I did everything I could to bring her back to the world of the living, but the truth was that I was the last person in the world to help her do that. I guess I was a little better than she was, but not by much. It was a half-hearted attempt."

"I'm so sorry," Lauren said. "I can't imagine…"

"Then, one day, my wife seemed to have changed. She was smiling and talking about how wonderful things were when the three of us traveled. She remembered the tiniest details that I had either forgotten or didn't know. All of my efforts to help my wife come out of her depression couldn't match the joy she had when she was diagnosed with terminal cancer. She'd gone to the doctor and didn't tell me right away, so I had no idea."

Horrified at his words, Lauren tried to make sense of what he was saying. "She wanted to die so she could be with Gia?"

He nodded. "That was it exactly. Chemo would only have given us a few more months together, not that it mattered to her. She would have refused treatment even if it would cure her."

"I guess there's a part of me that can understand her thinking," Lauren said.

He looked at her and smiled. "And this is where you come in, dear Lauren."

"I don't understand," she said.

"If you get me a taxi or an Uber, I'll explain."

CHAPTER 27

"Take a right here," Matteo instructed the driver as they slowly drove through the Fort Myers Memorial Gardens.

"Stop here," Matteo said..

The driver got out of the car and walked around to open the door, helping Matteo out of the car.

"Will you please wait?" Lauren asked the driver.

He nodded. "Of course."

Lauren put her arm through Matteo's as they walked toward the gravesite. They stood in front of a beautifully carved stone of flowers woven through a cross, his wife and daughter's names etched on the front.

The driver ran to them when he saw Matteo trying to lower himself to the ground.

"I'm all right. I can do this."

Lauren thanked the man and joined Matteo on the ground.

"I like to smell the earth. This will be my home soon," he said, smiling.

"Don't say that. You have plenty more time."

"No. I have stomach cancer. I got the news about nine months ago."

"Oh, I'm sorry, Mr.....Matteo. I'm so very sorry."

He shook his head. "Don't be. I finally understand how my wife felt when she was diagnosed. Anyway, let's not waste time talking about me. Did I tell you that my wife was an English teacher?"

Lauren shook her head. "No, you didn't."

"She loved being a teacher. She loved that, being a mother and gardening. She used to talk about what she was teaching the kids in her classroom. You should have seen her when she talked about them. Her face lit up like a Christmas tree."

Lauren laughed. "I wish I could have seen that."

They sat quietly for a few minutes and then Lauren spoke. "Can I ask you something?"

He nodded.

"Why are you sharing all this with me? I mean, don't get me wrong, I'm honored that you wanted to, but...well, you must have noticed that my mother, and everyone else back at the inn, have been wondering about you. Why haven't you told them your story?"

"Before my wife died, she made me promise her that I'd go back to every place we traveled as a family. She wanted me to celebrate the life we had and do it in her and Gia's memory. But, after she died, I couldn't do anything. I could barely get out of bed. You see, after Gia died, I had a terrible case of survivor's guilt. Why did Gia die and not me? In time, I was glad to not walk normally. I wanted the reminder of what a terrible parent I was."

"It wasn't your fault," Lauren said. "There was nothing you could do. You tried your hardest to save her. You..."

A lump formed in her throat, and tears welled in her eyes.

Matteo reached for her hand. "Yes, I know that now, but the years I wasted hating myself, and doubting my role as her father didn't help my wife or me or anyone who crossed our paths for a long time."

Lauren understood that doubt all too well.

"There was a fire at my business and several businesses that were attached to mine because of a new restaurant next door. Two young people...teenagers, died. My two employees and dear friends almost perished working for me. My baby...I put my baby at risk because I wanted to have a successful real estate business instead of putting my efforts into focusing on my family...my children. What kind of mother does that?"

"I doubt very much that you are a bad mother, Lauren. More to the point is that there was nothing you could do. You didn't start the fire. You were as much a victim of the situation as the kids who died. You could have died, but you didn't. You're still here. You and your child are alive. That's what you have to live for. Survivor's guilt is an awful thing. It eats away at your life and if you don't let it go, eventually, it will take your life."

Weeks of pretending that everything was fine had taken its toll on her. She was tired and leaned against the stone.

"You asked me why I shared this with you and no one else?"

She nodded.

"Along with my wife's request that I travel, she asked me one more thing. She said that our family had so much love. She said along my travels when I found someone who needed to hear our story, I should share it. Captiva Island was the last stop on our travels and my last stop as well. Until I reached this island, I hadn't found anyone with whom I could open the wounds of the accident and Gia's death. Not until I saw you yesterday."

"Yesterday?"

"Yes, you were sitting near the koi pond, all alone. I watched you stare into that pond as if it was nothing but a big, black hole. I don't even think you saw the fish swimming about. You picked up a rock from the path and rubbed it back and forth with your thumb, as if to soothe a pain deep inside. I knew then that I had to talk to you."

Holding his stomach, Matteo suddenly bent over, his face writhing in pain.

Lauren called to their driver for help. When he reached them, he and Lauren slowly lifted Matteo off the ground.

"We should get you to a hospital," she said.

His face wet with sweat, he shook his head. "No. No hospital. Get me back to the inn."

The Uber driver drove as quickly as he could without alerting a police cruiser. Lauren sent a text to her mother warning her of the situation.

When they reached the inn, Maggie and Paolo were waiting in the driveway.

"I'm fine. No need to make a fuss."

"Let's get you to your room," Paolo said.

Lauren paid the driver and thanked him. She then followed Matteo to his room.

"Honestly, I'm fine. This happens sometimes."

"What can I get you?" Maggie asked.

"A glass of water, please."

"Got it. I'll be right back."

Lauren leaned his cane against the nightstand, sat next to him and held his hand. "I think you did too much today. You should rest now. "

Maggie brought the water and Paolo waited for more instruction from her. "Should we call a doctor?" he whispered.

Lauren looked at Paolo. "No. He doesn't want a doctor. He needs to sleep for a while, that's all."

"Matteo, you call for someone if you need help. Don't try to get out of bed on your own. We'll bring your dinner to you when it's time."

"Thank you, Maggie. You too, Paolo. I appreciate it."

Lauren got up to follow Maggie and Paolo out of the room but Matteo grabbed her arm.

"Don't forget what we talked about, Lauren. Promise you won't forget."

She smiled and patted his hand. "I won't forget. You rest now."

Lauren closed his door and joined the others in the kitchen. She wanted to properly thank Matteo for sharing his story with her, but she needed time to find the right words…the ones that changed her and her baby's life, forever.

Surprised to see Grandma Sarah standing in front of her, Jacqui Hutchins apologized.

"Oh, I'm sorry. I didn't know Chelsea had company. I can come back another time."

"You don't remember me, do you?" Grandma asked.

"Um, no, I don't. Should I?"

"I'm Maggie Moretti's mother."

"Oh, right. I remember you. It's nice to see you again."

Chelsea appeared next to Grandma Sarah. "Hey, you, come on in. I see you've met Maggie's mother."

"Yes, we've met. I didn't mean to disturb, I just wanted to run something by you, but we can do this another time."

"Nonsense. Let's go out on the lanai. We can talk out there," Chelsea said.

"You two pretend I'm not here," Grandma said.

Jacqui didn't know the woman well, but somehow she doubted that Grandma Sarah would ever be impossible to ignore.

"Can I get you something to drink?" Chelsea asked.

"No, I'm fine. Thanks."

Pulling up two wicker chairs, Chelsea sat across from Jacqui. "So, how have you been? I've heard about your father. I'm so sorry he's going through that. How is he doing?"

"Much better actually. He's regaining his speech. It's slow but he's able to communicate, which is good. He initially had paralysis on one side, but that is gone now. He has a strong constitution I think. This stroke probably would have killed anyone else."

Chelsea laughed at that. "Sounds like Devon all right."

"My brother Wyatt is home and he's joined Clayton and Trevor in running things at the company. So far they haven't killed each other so that's progress. Anyway, as you know I've just graduated and now I'm trying to figure out where I should live and work. It's hard because I've been torn between staying in New York and coming back home to Florida."

"I don't know which way you're leaning, but if I were a young woman about to start my life as an artist, I'd stay in New York."

"I was afraid you were going to say that," Jacqui said.

"I see. You don't think that's a good idea?"

"It's absolutely a good idea...it's the practical, logical, and appropriate answer."

"But?"

"But, there's Joshua Powell. He's here on Captiva still working at Powell Water Sports."

Chelsea nodded. "Well, it is his family's business and, from what I've heard, a business that both he and his brother Luke plan to inherit and grow. I don't see him moving to New York, even if he is in love."

Jacqui's face lit up. "Do you think he's in love? Did he say that?"

Chelsea laughed. "Honey, calm down. I have not heard him say so specifically, but Ciara definitely thinks so and she's about to become his step-mother, so I think she'd know better than any of us."

"So, I'm not only considering staying in Florida just for Joshua. I have another idea and that's why I'm here. What if you and I team up and do something like open a gallery? In addition to the gallery, we could also teach kids or adults how to paint?"

"Team up? Me and you? Oh, sweetie, that is very nice of you to consider me. I mean, let's not ignore the fact that I'm old enough to be your mother, and..."

"You're old enough to be her grandmother," Grandma Sarah yelled from the kitchen.

"If you're planning on eavesdropping, perhaps you'll bring out some iced tea for all of us and pull up a chair," Chelsea yelled back.

Not more than ten seconds passed before Grandma Sarah sat at the table with them. Pouring two more glasses of iced tea she handed them to Chelsea and Jacqui. "Listen, do you have anything else going on in your life?" Grandma asked Chelsea.

Giving Grandma a threatening stare, Chelsea said, "I'll handle this."

Grandma Sarah pinched two fingers together and slid them from one side of her mouth to the other. Her imaginary zipper fooled no one.

Turning to Jacqui, Chelsea continued. "First, you don't just decide one day to open a gallery and poof, artists show up. It takes money and..."

"I've got money," Jacqui said.

"It takes getting your name out there in the art world."

"You've already got a reputation for being an amazing artist and you've already had showings of your work. Trust me, your name is out there," Jacqui insisted.

Grandma Sarah sat stoically, her face not making eye contact with anyone but Jacqui could feel the woman was chomping at the bit to say something.

"What?" Jacqui asked her.

Grandma looked at Chelsea for permission to speak.

"Go ahead. It's not like I can stop you."

"I think you don't have anything to lose. Jacqui is willing to put up the money, and if it fails then she goes back to New York and you're not out a thing. But, if it's a success, just think how much fun you'll have."

Jacqui smiled at Grandma Sarah. "Way to go, Grandma!"

Chelsea rolled her eyes. "You say that now, but you should know this woman just bought a condo not a stone's throw from here. She's not going anywhere, anytime soon, and she's never heard the term, 'mind your own business.'"

"I've got to get back to my father. I'm having dinner with him tonight. Sleep on this and I'll stop by tomorrow. We can talk more about it."

She turned to Grandma Sarah. "Nice to talk with you, Grandma. I hope I get to see you again soon."

Chelsea shook her head. "Oh, you will. I can guarantee it."

CHAPTER 28

Maggie felt overwhelmed as she looked over her 'to-do' list. Going to Italy for a wedding meant that she'd need several outfits she wouldn't normally pack. The last time she had to think about formalwear was on a cruise she and Daniel took a year before he died. Living on Captiva Island, Maggie loved living in shorts and beach attire most of the time.

She'd set out several combinations of tops and bottoms and mixed and matched colors until she couldn't spend one more minute adjusting. When she'd had enough, she folded everything and filled her luggage.

She wanted to check with Ciara about what to wear this time of year in her hometown, but she and Crawford had already left the day before. Throwing caution to the wind, she'd have to be happy with however she looked.

"Mom, are you up there?" Lauren called out.

"I'm here. Come on up."

"You're finally getting around to packing."

"I am, indeed. I loved having the girls here, but the whole time I kept thinking about all the things I had to do before we left for

Italy. I might add that I'm so grateful to you for helping your grandmother out. I worried that I'd only be able to spend a few hours with her the day of the move. This gives me the freedom to get ready for our trip. What can I do to thank you? Let Paolo and I take you out for a delicious dinner someplace nice...your pick."

"My pick?"

Maggie nodded. "Absolutely." She then lifted the luggage off the bed and began organizing her purse.

"Then I choose right here with you and a nice hot cup of tea."

Maggie looked at Lauren and saw the light that had been missing for so long.

"Mommy," she said as she ran into Maggie's arms.

"Oh, my baby," Maggie said, holding Lauren as close as ever. "My baby. Can you forgive me?"

Lauren pulled back and looked at her mother. "Forgive you? I need you to forgive me for being so awful and distant."

"Come, let's go into the living room and sit," Maggie said.

Just then, Maggie heard Paolo climbing the stairs to join them. "Can you come back later?"

"What?" he asked but seemed to understand better when he saw the two women crying. He turned and ran down the stairs faster than he had climbed them.

"Lauren, honey, I should have jumped on a plane and left everything behind when I heard about the fire. I'm so sorry that I didn't go to you."

Lauren shook her head. "No, Mom, that's not fair. I think even if you did fly up, I might not have been able to talk to you or even listen to anything you had to say. I wasn't ready. I didn't realize it at the time, but I know it now."

Maggie needed to hear what was in Lauren's heart. "Honey, why do you think that is?"

"I've struggled with knowing that my baby, and Nell and Brian, almost died."

"And you too, silly. You might have died too."

"Yes, I know, when those two kids died, I felt so awful. I guess it's what they call survivor's guilt. The only problem was that if I was feeling guilty about being alive, what did that mean for my baby? I was so disconnected from this child and I hated myself for it. I didn't want anyone around me. I couldn't make eye contact with anyone for fear that I'd see disappointment in their eyes. Especially you. You're the best mother in the world. I couldn't compete."

"Oh, Lauren. I'm so sorry you've been dealing with this. You must have felt so alone. But, baby, you're not alone. You have me and everyone in this family has been worried sick about you. Did you know that? Michael, Christopher, Beth, Sarah and Paolo and me. Your family could never be disappointed in you…ever."

For the first time since the fire, Lauren cried uncontrollably, but she did so right where she belonged…in her mother's arms.

Riley carried the tray of food to Matteo's room. She first knocked but when there was no answer she opened his door a crack.

"Mr. Benedetti, I've got your dinner."

Entering the room she could see that he was still sleeping, so she put the tray on the desk.

"I'll just leave it on the desk and when you're ready…"

His face was bluish-white and his mouth was open.

"Millie, go get Maggie and Paolo," she yelled out.

"Can it wait a minute, I'm…"

"No, it can't. Go get them now."

Millie stopped to look into Matteo's room. "Is he…?"

Riley nodded. "I think so."

Millie ran out of the building and across to the carriage house. When she got there Maggie and Lauren were the only ones there.

"Maggie, come quick, I think Mr. Benedetti is dead."

"What?" Maggie asked.

"I don't know. Riley brought him his dinner and when she went into the room, she found him."

"Go get Paolo. He's around somewhere."

Millie nodded and ran down the stairs. Maggie could hear her calling Paolo's name.

"I can't believe this," Maggie said.

"I can," Lauren said, a faint smile forming. Now he can really live."

"Who do we call? He didn't leave any instructions on what to do. He must have known this was a possibility," Paolo said.

"Wait. I have an idea. Remember his photo album? He let me look at it," Lauren said.

"He did?" Maggie asked. "Why did he..."

"I'll explain later, but what I remember is there was an envelope taped at the back of it on the inside. He left it in the garden. I'll go get it."

Lauren ran to the garden, found the photo album and returned to the kitchen with it. Everyone surrounded her, watching. She pulled the envelope off and opened it. Inside was one piece of paper explaining his wishes.

Lauren read it aloud.

To: The Key Lime Garden Inn Family

If you are reading this then my time has come. I'm sorry to have caused you so much distress. I hope you can be content knowing that in my last days you gave me comfort and kindness. Everyone should have as much when they are about to die.

I don't live very far from Captiva, but, for private reasons I stayed away as it held both happiness and heartache for me.

I finally confronted that heartache for the last time with this visit and have made peace with it.

Thank you.

Please call my brother Ralph at this number: 239-555-2040. He will know what to do.

"I'll make the call," Paolo said.

Diana was sitting on the back porch swing when everyone came out and joined her.

"Riley told me about Mr. Benedetti. I can't believe he died. He was such a sweet man."

"He was so kind to me. He always had a pleasant way about him, and it was so strange the way he seemed to know what I was thinking," Riley said.

"That's how I felt too," Millie added. "I was really feeling down and by the time he was done talking to me I felt so much better."

Paolo came out onto the porch. "Ralph said he'd be right over. He's called the coroner and they are on their way as well."

"Millie, will you get Mr. Benedetti's things from his room and have them ready for his brother? Make sure his photo album is there."

Millie nodded. "Sure thing."

"I feel awful. It feels like a family member has died," Maggie said. "Lauren, where were you today?"

Lauren explained everything to the group, leaving out Matteo's reason for sharing his story with her. "I guess he must have felt his time was near and wanted someone to talk to about it all at the very end."

It was the best Lauren could come up with. She felt a strong need to keep private her own struggles…struggles that only Matteo Benedetti had understood.

Ralph Benedetti was much younger looking than his brother, at least that's what Maggie thought. As it turned out, Ralph was Matteo's older brother.

Years of sadness over his daughter's death had taken its toll on Matteo, along with his wife's depression and finally stomach cancer, he looked much older than his years.

Ralph shook Paolo's hand. "Thank you for everything you did for my brother."

"Of course. We're so sorry for your loss. Matteo was a special person and all our lives have been forever changed for knowing him."

The coroner took Matteo's body away, and Ralph got in his car and placed the photo album on the passenger seat.

Everyone stood in the driveway unable to move. The entire event was so disturbing there wasn't much to do but go home or to bed, hoping to feel a little better the next day.

"I'm going back to Chelsea's" Lauren said "I'll see you all in the morning."

Maggie hugged Lauren and squeezed her tight. "Good night honey."

Grandma Sarah dragged Chelsea and Lauren out of bed before sunrise the next morning.

"This is the last day I will have to irritate you. Get up and let's get on the beach. I called Maggie too. She's going to meet us. I've made a nice big pot of coffee and put out insulated cups, sugar and creamer. Let's go."

It was indeed the last day as Lauren and Grandma Sarah would meet the movers the next day. Grandma wanted to make the most of it.

"Is she always like this?" Chelsea asked Lauren.

"Always. I've been dealing with this kind of thing all my life, but after tomorrow, she'll be your problem...and Mom's, of course."

They got dressed and headed to the kitchen.

Lauren yawned. "At least she made coffee."

"I can't wait to hear what your mother has to say about this. I'm surprised we can't hear her voice all the way from here."

After they'd filled their cups, the women walked to the beach, flip flops in hand.

Grandma Sarah took several deep breaths.

"Smell that ocean air. Isn't it wonderful? My condo isn't that far from here so I expect I'll be making early morning walks on the beach a regular thing."

"Thanks for the warning," Chelsea mumbled under her breath.

As they got closer to the Key Lime Garden Inn they could see Maggie heading toward them.

"Good morning, Maggie dear. I'm glad you could join us. It's good to keep moving, and I've noticed you've gained a few pounds since I last saw you."

"I move all day, Mom. I'm pretty sure I don't need to move right now."

"Wait, I thought you took early morning walks all the time. Why are you complaining?" her mother asked.

"I'm not complaining, and yes, I do take walks, but we all went through a very traumatic situation yesterday and I'm not in a very good mood this morning."

Grandma Sarah stopped walking and waited for the others to do the same.

"Maggie Garrison Wheeler Moretti..."

Maggie rolled her eyes. "Great. Here it comes."

"Don't you dare let Mr. Benedetti's death be in vain. From everything I've heard about that man, he gave each and every one of you instructions on how to live. He shared his life with you all and warned you not to spend your days lamenting things you have no control over. Now, get your body moving and stop fussing."

Maggie hugged her mother. "You're right. I'm sorry. Let's go."

Chelsea took a sip of her coffee and did her best to suppress a giggle. Now that Maggie's mother was living nearby, she imagined many such conversations in the coming months.

They walked almost three miles before Grandma Sarah finally ended their torture.

When they were done they followed the aroma that was coming from the inn's kitchen.

"All that exercise made me hungry," Chelsea said.

Maggie nodded. "Me too. I'm starving. Let's go see what Riley's made for breakfast."

They walked through the beach path and the flower garden. As they continued toward the porch stairs, Lauren stopped.

"You guys go on ahead. I'll be right there."

She watched the others go inside before turning and walking past the rose bushes, flower beds and butterfly bush. Following the stone path, she continued toward the koi pond and the tree where she'd found Matteo sitting on the ground only the day before.

She stopped and smiled. There, leaning against the tree, was his cane.

THE END

Thank you for reading Return to Captiva. Reviews are very important to authors. If you've enjoyed this story, please feel free to leave a review. I love to hear from my readers.

This book was to be the last in the Captiva Island series, however, after much demand, I have decided that there will be several more books about The Wheeler family.
I hope you will return with me to Southwest Florida and the island I love so much in 2024.

ALSO BY ANNIE CABOT

THE CAPTIVA ISLAND SERIES

Book One: KEY LIME GARDEN INN

Book Two: A CAPTIVA WEDDING

Book Three: CAPTIVA MEMORIES

Book Four: CAPTIVA CHRISTMAS

Book Five: CAPTIVA NIGHTS

Book Six: CAPTIVA HEARTS

Book Seven: CAPTIVA EVER AFTER

Book Eight: CAPTIVA HIDEAWAY

For a **FREE** copy of the Prequel to the Captiva Island Series, **Captiva Sunset** - Join my newsletter HERE.

THE PERIWINKLE SHORES SERIES

Book One: CHRISTMAS ON THE CAPE

Book Two: THE SEA GLASS GIRLS

ACKNOWLEDGMENTS

With each book I continue to be grateful to the people who support my work. I couldn't do what I do without them. Thank you all so much.

Cover Design: Marianne Nowicki
Premade Ebook Cover Shop
https://www.premadeebookcovershop.com/

Editor: Lisa Lee of Lisa Lee Proofreading and Editing
https://www.facebook.com/EditorLisaLee/

Beta Readers:
John Battaglino
Nancy Burgess
Michele Connolly
Anne Marie Page Cooke

ABOUT THE AUTHOR

Annie Cabot is the author of contemporary women's fiction and family sagas. Annie writes about friendships and family relationships, that bring inspiration and hope to others.

Annie Cabot is the pen name for the writer Patricia Pauletti (Patti) who was a co-author of several paranormal mystery books under the pen name Juliette Harper.

A lover of all things happily ever after, it was only a matter of time before she began to write what was in her heart, and so, the pen name Annie Cabot was born.

When she's not writing, Annie and her husband like to travel. Winters always involve time away on Captiva Island, Florida where she continues to get inspiration for her novels.

Annie lives in Massachusetts with her husband and an adorable new puppy named Willa.

For more information visit anniecabot.com

Made in the USA
Columbia, SC
21 November 2024